Lord Thayer's Choice

Lords and Little Ladies Book 1
By Alyssa Bailey

Description

S addles and tobacco are not all they are selling in the shops today.

Annalise Coton is to be sold to the highest bidder. At eighteen, she has met her usefulness as a nursemaid to her half-brother. With no natural parent to protect her from the outcome, she will go home with the man offering the best price by the close of business today. Proposal of marriage optional.

But if the choice were hers, the attractive lord who entered the leather shop is the one she would consider. He was obviously used to having his desires met, but there was a gentleness about him that belied the harder, angular exterior. She imagined he would be a strict taskmaster, possibly a ruffian in the marriage bed, but a tender caretaker. She would go with him if he would only pay her price.

Lord Stephen Thayer needed to find a wife, produce heirs, and meet his first-son obligations. Which was fine, however, he had prerequisites that were making a choice difficult, and he would not lower his expectations or standards merely to obtain a bride. Stephen wasn't a snob. He had needs, and he wanted a woman who had the same desires as he did, but how to find her was the issue. With the London season ended, Stephen prepares to return to his estate, stopping to purchase some needed leather and possibly a new pistol. He finds that a new saddle and pistol are not all that is offered at the shops today.

He wants a burst of sunshine in the morning, a sprite in the afternoon, a lady in the evening, and a wanton at night, but the choic-

1

es are slim. Are his desires unattainable? Could the lovely blonde-haired sprite with the biting tongue, innocent bravado, and enticing pout be the answer to his dilemma? Would she submit to his benevolent manner and subtle take-charge ways? The choice was his to make and hers to take.

Love the inside scoop? Sign up for my Newsletter with special offers and bonus content.

https://www.alyssabaileyromance.com

Chapter 1

Lord Stephen Thayer entered the ballroom to survey his last event of the autumn season. He had reluctantly agreed to host the final soirée to please his parents. Now he totally understood the feelings that his sister, Georgiana, proclaimed loud and clear when she was coming out three years ago. These young women, some no more than girls embarking on their first season, were on the auction block. He had rolled his eyes at the dramatic rendition, but now he agreed wholeheartedly. In his sister's case, the result of such a marketing frenzy was that she was happily ensconced in a beautiful estate, awaiting their first child with the proclaimed love of her life.

That's what Stephen wanted. He wanted to be done with the chase. Unlike when he took his hunting dogs to flush the pheasants from the tall reeds on his shoot, the perfect targets did not present themselves. It appeared his family was less able to uncover the better choices for a wife with his desires in mind than he had been when first approaching the task. Their idea of requirements was fine, but they didn't align with his own. This evening would be the last push before the winter began in earnest, and his efforts to find a wife lessened considerably for half a year.

Who would have known how trying it would be to find a woman to share his name? One who would also not be opposed to filling his nursery and his desires? It's not that Stephen was only interested in producing an heir. In fact, that was the problem. He made it clear that he wasn't only interested in procreating the requisite heir and a spare, but he wanted more. How did he get to this place? He had position, money, and title and until recently, no desire to ferret out the perfect mate.

"I'm not inclined to be leg shackled until I am ready," was an acceptable stance that he fervently held, until this year.

However, he had completed the formal season without a wife, and now he was closing the short autumn season without a bride. The trouble was that Lord Thayer wanted it all. He wanted a wife who was elegant and presented well, thus ensuring his standing in society. He wanted that same woman to tear down all of her barriers and be quite a wildcat in his bedchamber. One who gave the appearance of a woman uninterestingly proper in public but behind closed doors was adventuresome, passionate, and not at all prudish.

Finally, he wanted that lovely lady to allow him to pamper her when the need struck him. Not indulge as with jewels and dresses, for he would do that automatically, but with his time and attentions. To play and allow him to coddle her, nurture her as a papa would. As his bride, allow him to bind her to his bed, make her scream his name in the agony of undiluted pleasure.

He wanted her to be wanton on one day and needy as a child on another. He wanted a vixen in bed in the morning, innocent submission mid-day, and the consummate hostess in the evening. Upon retiring of an evening, the love of his life would revert back to the adventuresome vixen.

After speaking to a gentleman at his club some months ago, Stephen felt that he could, at last, relax in his proclivities. "It is roleplaying, much as actors and actresses, exploring their character. I hear women love the pretense even more than their men. It is a fact that mine does."

Stephen ordered another drink. "Is it always? And why is that do you think?"

"I can only speak for my wife and myself. But my position brings with it many responsibilities that fall onto my wife. I imagine yours does as well. My wife becomes distraught when she is exceedingly weary or overtaxed, but an afternoon or evening as my ward, or as my naughty little school miss, seems to rejuvenate us both."

He also explained that if there were corrections necessary, he most typically dealt out that correction in this particular role. There were times that his wife needed to relieve her stress, and it was according to what that stress was and where it originated from as to whether she was his lady, his lover, or his little one when the relief occurred.

Stephen thought about the possibility quite often since that conversation and found that it made much more sense to him than any of the other scenarios presented thus far. He had spent a little time formulating the type of woman who would fulfill such a particular genre of desires on occasion. The list seemed formidable, and quite frankly, unattainable, for how could one ask a woman if she would allow or shared certain tendencies, such as allowing her husband to smack her arse?

Another friend put it in another light. "Thayer, you put your efforts into finding a woman who will be submissive to your desires that you also, hopefully, have an obvious affection and the rest will happen however it happens. You will be glad of the outcome, I promise. At that juncture, it will matter not whether your preconceived ideas of your particular needs are met, because you will be happy.

If she is happy with you, she will try to please you because it will please her. As it will be the same with you. If you think you desire a type of bondage and she is not prepared to be bound, you accept it and, through patience, try to entice her. However, it is the woman herself, which matters first and foremost. You will be able to see the right one if that is what you put your focus on."

Unfortunately, this evening, as in all others thus far, he found there weren't many available women who took his kind of bait.

Stephen looked around at the room full of visually enticing women, all casting their glances his way. Some women looked boldly, some tentatively, but all looking his way and all falling short of their goal and his. He wasn't a difficult man to look upon, and many a woman commented on his deep blue eyes and dark chocolate hair. He was of a height that complemented most woman and took care with his build and grooming.

The parade of young women who strutted before him this evening, since the announcement that he was officially looking for a bride, was astounding. He straightened himself, for yet another presentation was coming his way. She appeared to be a comely young woman and possibly someone he could consider.

"My Lord Thayer," gushed the young woman's mother, "this is my daughter, Ophelia. I do not believe the two of you have been made known to the other." Stephen indicated that they had not, and that was enough encouragement for this matron to continue. Where was the girl's father? "Yes, well, you will be happy to know her father, Lord Grantham, was desirous that I facilitate a meeting if you did not already know each other. I was quite sure you had not exchanged conversation."

When it came time for the young lady to speak, there was silence, a substantial silence worthy of a cricket serenade. Maybe she needed encouragement.

"Yes, splendid, thank you. And, Lady Ophelia, I pray the season has gone well for you?" It was a well-used question and yet there was no answer forthcoming. Apparently, this young woman's parent felt encouraged to speak for her and did so rather incessantly.

"Oh, my Lord Thayer, you can't imagine what she has done this season. My Ophelia has gone to every event possible and been to the theater twice. She has engaged in walks in the Commons, and then in Hyde Park during the fashionable hours, of course." Her tone changed to one of slight chastisement. "However, we've not seen you there once, my lord."

"Yes, I don't do that."

"Don't do what, my lord?"

"Strut or trot in a circle, my dear madam. I must say that even as a young man, the 'fashionable' hour never impressed me. In fact, if that is what is essential to a woman, she needs to find a gentleman who she encounters there in the parks, for it obviously would be important to him as well."

While he was very careful not to be snide, this hopeful candidate had said not one word since she had approached him with her matron. The girl sniffed her disapproval of his sentiment, but that was all. Was she mute or possibly addled he wondered? He had no time for a woman who couldn't speak her own mind. Nor did he have time for a girl whose mother spoke for her. He couldn't even imagine the horrors of that connection. He bid the women well, stifled a yawn, and excused himself, never once having an idea of what Lady Ophelia even sounded like.

He recounted the incident to his brother James, who laughed and shook his head. "I don't know, Stephen. You might've looked at that one a bit harder. She is comely, her mother doesn't have a hugely horrible reputation yet for throwing her daughter at every available man of peerage, and a wife who doesn't argue might be an asset."

"Yes, I can see how you might think that, given your in-laws. However, a wife who speaks not at all except through her mother would be an even worse predicament. I prefer to have my wife speak her mind even if a bit too much, rather than she does not speak at all." He bid a pleasant evening to his sister-in-law, who was looking askance at her husband as she tightened her grip on James' arm. With an amused smile, Lord Thayer resumed his duties as host and started a new sweep of the room.

Stephen was heard to describe things as "naughty" and "wicked" causing many a blush to rise up a cheek, but not a one challenged his questionably inappropriate choice of words, no spunk. Conversely, none gave a look of enjoying the exchange either, no spice. Embarrassment and astonishment were all he encountered. He referred to several hopefuls as "little one" and "mischievous" looking for a response.

A couple of bright, attractive young women seemed intrigued by his odd usage of words but failed miserably to take the bait upon further luring, their faces taking on the scandalized look of their peers. Not as much as even a spark of interest or acceptance, dared he hope delight. All evening, he tried to find an affinity that could lead to affection, but no one presented.

Stephen struck up a conversation with several gentlemen, and within the span of that short discourse, no less than three mamas brought up their daughters to meet him. One woman had two daughters and wanted him to consider both of them. He was quite sure she didn't mean at the same time. However, he was left with the unclear understanding that she might indeed give him both were Stephen of that persuasion. To be done with the greatest of discretion, of course.

By the end of the evening, Stephen was swearing an oath of retribution upon his parents who felt that this small announcement at his soirée would be just the ticket to find the woman of his dreams. He was quite confident that after this evening's debacle, nightmares were all that would accompany him to bed from this lot. He was quite certain that while several of them took his fancy for a moment; he didn't believe they could meet all the requirements he needed from his wife. He felt he would know her instinctively. There would be a spark.

As the last guest exited his home that evening, Stephen was disheartened. It was indeed a horrid night, one that seemed to sap him of all his energy. His social attributes had been put to the ultimate test, and while he felt he maintained throughout, there might have been a question for the last hour. His inner male intuition, that he had been assured his whole life would be the determiner of which young lady he should choose, had either not worked or had been overused by the end of the evening. He truly was weary in mind, body, and soul.

After deciding that one more polite thought or conversation would entirely destroy the inner workings of his mind, Stephen went to bed immediately after his last guest left for home. The one thing that he enjoyed about being in the city was no one needed to stay over as everyone else was also in the city. If he had to undergo such a trying but necessary ordeal as this evening, at least they all went home at the conclusion of the party.

Stephen stared out the window of his private sitting room and thought of his predicament. There must have been forty unattached women there tonight. From mousy baggage just out of the school-room to well-established women who should have long found their husband, causing one to wonder why they had not. Widows were wandering the rooms all evening and not one with the ability to turn his head, at least not for long. He went to bed exhausted and unsatisfied.

The conversation in the study before his father left for the country the next morning resonated with him. When it came down to choosing a life partner, he was quite serious about his decision. He would not just choose anyone. The position he was offering entailed being his companion as well. He wanted more than an alliance in name only. He knew that was not a popular viewpoint among his peers and many of his mates laughed at him, and yet he continued stalwartly with that end goal in mind.

He did feel the pressure of time, however, for his father, as recently as this morning, had pointed out to him that he didn't want to be in his dotage before he had grandchildren his eldest son had sired. When Stephen mentioned that dotage meant the age of doting of which a grandparent would qualify, his father pooh-poohed him and said, "Find a wife."

"Stephen, you've got to put away your unrealistic expectations and settle on a wife. I know there are not many who would draw your eye, but there are some. Fix on one of them and let us be done with the bloody games."

"I know you are right, Father, but I do have to like the woman. I'm not sure why a comely face and a good background are not enough, but it isn't."

He knew but would not disclose the real reason to his father. What Stephen wanted to say was, "I would prefer to be a papa to my wife as well as husband and lover." Instead, he responded, "There needs to be a spark of some kind, and preferably a brain of some measure as well. I cannot have a reason-deficient wife no matter her level of manners. She cannot rely on me for every thought and choice. I would go mad."

His father softened his tone. "I know how hard it is to make a decision, but you could always find a paramour once you have your heirs, sooner if she is so distasteful, but it is your responsibility as my heir to ensure the lineage."

His father was right, of course. It was time to start his nursery. James did not have the same concerns, as he was the second son. Stephen's responsibility was laid out before him. He was not a hard man to please, but he did have some standards that he felt reticent to ignore. He reasoned with himself it was not that his standards were exceedingly high, elevated yes, extraordinarily so, no. He simply needed to extend his search.

Stephen was soon to depart to the country for winter as well, but he had a few more loose ends to tie up, so his father and brother were taking their families back home several days earlier than Stephen had planned to go. James and Elizabeth were having their second child, and she was soon to show her condition, so they felt it better that she did so in the country.

His brother entered the room and joined the conversation while waiting for Elizabeth to complete her packing. "So how fairs the hunt? Bagged any you'd care to share about?"

Stephen gave his brother a mischievous grin. "We aren't all so easily taken by beauty."

James shook his head and smiled in gest. "Not a moment's regret."

"Except for the parents she brought with her." Stephen waited for his brother to deny the obvious.

"Yes, except for them." James frowned good naturedly.

"Stephen, are there any women who have even piqued your interest in the slightest way?" asked his father.

"Well, not that Landry woman. Gad, her manners are atrocious, absolutely astonishing." The three men sat with ale that had silently appeared with an attentive footman, to contemplate further Stephen's fate.

"There is no help for it, but she guffaws," continued Stephen. "I cannot, will not, live with a laughing horse."

"Stephen, be kind, son," Lord Thayer admonished. "Although, I must agree with your assessment. Don't tell your mother. She's rather taken with the woman."

James added to the conversation, "Now Lady Roundtree is interesting."

"Yes, James," Stephen agreed, "very fair to look at, but then I danced with her, and discovered she has very little to support an original thought."

"Oh? Shame, that. Her children would have been handsome," observed his father.

Stephen laughed. "Yes, however, I suppose I should find occasion to speak to the woman I choose to marry, not simply bed her."

"Pity. Then what about that blonde you danced with last night?" James asked. "She was comely, and you were laughing and speaking quite well with her."

His father joined in, "Oh yes, that was the Donnelly lass? She would have plenty of strong children."

"Yes, but she was quite clear about being desirous of Lord Madison. As a gentleman, I should not usurp that option from her."

"Yes, it wouldn't do. You'd have an immediate discord. Better not to start out with any," pointed out James. "Lady Johnstone?"

His father replied dryly, "Hips too narrow. How about the recent widow Lady Aaron?" "Too many children. I do want some of my own."

"Lady Winchesterly?" suggested James.

James snorted. "Too tiresome and too jaded."

"I'm not sure I have much more to help you with, brother."

"I know. I'll find one. I am not a particular man," he said, to which his companions laughed in disbelief. He continued defensively, "There are just some things a man cannot forfeit, and peace of mind is one of those things. Affection is another attribute he should not sacrifice."

"Yes, well, I hope it keeps you warm at night. That peace of mind."

Stephen turned to his brother. "How did you choose Elizabeth?"

"She was everything I wanted. I didn't have to decide; the choice was already made when I met her."

"Yes, well, too bad your Elizabeth came with a mother cut from a different cloth. Don't tell your mother that either." Their father spoke churlishly.

"Quite right. Father, how about you with mother? How did you know?" asked James.

"The moment I danced with her, I knew. The minute she stomped her small foot at me in agitation, I made the deal. I knew she was perfect."

"Well, then I shall look for a woman who is not too long in the tooth, but not a schoolgirl, with a brain but not a bluestocking, one who can make me laugh but not rudely so. She must have ample hips, stomping feet, with manners. She must have a rounded arse for spanking and no more than two added strap-hangers. Let's see, anyone come to mind?"

"Sorry, old man, I don't think that girl exists." Both men sadly mumbled no prospects in their memory.

"Well then, that means I close up the house and go to the country for the winter entertainment, and maybe I'll find someone in the New Year."

While he changed some of his requirements as the search continued, the one thing Lord Thayer had not deviated from since he'd begun his search was a wife who could run his house as Lady Thayer with precision and confidence. He wanted her wanton in his bedchambers, one who was insatiable and desperate for his touch.

It was desirable that a woman who would eventually give him an heir or three because she chose to, would be an asset in every part of his life. While children were desired and a necessity, he didn't want one without the other. He wanted it all. Lastly, he wanted one who could place in his hands her insecurities, her needs, and her trust that he could and would keep her safe and happy forever.

Several days later found Lord Thayer at the conclusion of all of his London business. In celebration of returning home, Stephen decided to have a look at the shops near his city home one last time, to see if there was anything that he might have need of that would be more difficult to acquire in his little shire.

Therefore, once breakfast was over, he gathered his coat and gloves, for the weather was quite blustery, got into the carriage, and headed into town. He brought along his valet, who also needed to obtain things in town for his lordship. Stephen had become quite restless and disgruntled as of late. He had been to the balls and countless soirées where every mother in known society had paraded their daughters in front of him trying to entice his selection to no avail. It had continued even to this morning when a hopeful's father had called on him. His valet announced today, as he was helping his lordship dress, that he had become heartily sick of the routine and was glad they were done with the lot.

"Speaking rather boldly, aren't you? I will continue to do what I see fit and necessary for the good of my family and myself. Is there more you need to discuss on this subject?"

"What? Oh, I beg your forgiveness, my lord. I misspoke."

Thayer sighed. "No, you were truthful, and I can't say that I blame you, but keeping a civil tongue when I am at sixes and sevens with a mood to match would be a prudent idea, don't you think?"

"Yes, milord, absolutely. I apologize for speaking carelessly."

"No harm is done."

Stephen was a rather intelligent man who had significant holdings thanks to his family's good business sense. Business sense that he had inherited. He had searched for a wife in great earnest using that sound logic, but he wondered if he had gone about things in too calculated a manner.

He wanted children, and the settled home that so many of his contemporaries had. He was tired of being the one who his friends' wives were matchmaking for and the one who was forever having carrots dangled before his eyes. Or sweetmeats according to the dangler's status. Maybe he needed to strategize less and just let things happen. He was a calculated thinker, and just letting things happen by chance was something he didn't do well, if at all.

As they neared the shops, Stephen took an interest in the people on the street. He was not a snob, per se. However, there was a certain way that the upper classes were taught to behave that would look quite arrogant to most, but to each other, it was simply the way it was. You told no one of your inner secrets because inner secrets ruined people. Everyone had things they needed to keep quiet, just as his secret could easily bring him down, which was why very few in the world knew of his proclivities, and those who knew were bound by the same bindings as he.

Pushing that all out of his mind, Lord Thayer conversed with his valet until they reached the merchant shops. Reggie, his head groomsman, had ridden in to pick out new tack and leather for the repairing of old equipment. Stephen wanted to choose a new saddle. He also liked to look at the guns available. Seeing the leather shop next to the gunsmith shop and the tobacco shop on the other side of that, Lord Thayer indicated that's where he wanted to stop. It looked like the perfect male shopping. His valet went down a bit further to avail himself of gentlemen's accessories that his lordship would need when he was returned to the country.

"I should stop in and look at the saddles now so that you can make arrangements to get them home, Reggie," said Stephen once he had stepped out of the carriage. The brisk air was a bit of a shock after sitting in the cozier carriage replete with hot stones and blankets. There looked to be quite a brisk business going on in the gun shop next door. Stephen hoped that it would die down while he was in the tack shop.

The smell of leather permeated the establishment, relaxing Stephen with its familiar scent. He had hoped that he would be buying tack for his new wife, but it was not to be, not on this trip anyway. He felt the leathers, some well worked, some stiff and unyielding. He enjoyed working the leather, making it supple and warm.

The variety of tack was broad, and Stephen found himself lost in the exploration in search of something unique. He often looked for small strips of leather inadequate for tack. He had begun tooling his own implements, just as fishing lures, or hunting arrows. It was a good winter pastime in front of the fire. One his future wife would have input if - so desired.

He left Reggie to figure out the things that he was best at after having chosen a well-tooled riding crop, and a soft deer leather flogger. He hesitated to get the flogger, but he thought he would add it to his implements, for he did not give up hope that he would be able to find someone who would love its use as much as he would love to use it.

"I'll leave you to it then, Reggie," signaled Lord Thayer. "Don't forget to find me some scraps of leather."

"Aye, milord, shall I take it and go when I'm done here?" asked Reggie, his voice rich with a Scot's lilt.

"That would be fine. And take these two things," added Lord Thayer as he handed Reggie the brown paper-wrapped package. "Have them placed in my chambers."

"Aye."

Stephen braced himself to leave the tight warm shop to step back out into the clear but frigid air in search of a pistol when a young woman entered.

Chapter 2

Annalise stood in front of the gray and cracked mirror, trying to get a good look at herself. She ran her fingers through her tangle of hair in an attempt to tame its wildness. She had long since given up on her looks as she had never anticipated attracting a husband worth grooming for, but now that the day had come to leave her home, she lamented the loss of her brush. That wasn't all that she grieved.

She mourned the loss of her mother years ago, and she bemoaned the marriage of her mother to this man whom Annalise must show honor to as her stepfather. Regardless of the fact that he was merely the male who married her matron for her money, it was expected. Her mother had died soon after giving birth to her half-brother, Julius, six years ago. She also knew only too well that she mourned the loss of her hopes and dreams, however small they may have become. They were hers, nonetheless.

Annalise brought her thoughts back to today and wondered if she had time to rinse out her dress, but decided dirty and dry was better than wet, cold, and clean. She had been expecting this day for quite a while but had been shocked nonetheless when it happened. Her stepfather had walked in this morning and told her that she was eighteen now and needed to go and live with her husband. Annalise didn't think it was prudent to point out that she had no male callers, gentleman or otherwise. Nor had she had an eye for any man at all and, therefore, held her tongue.

She marveled that he had walked in just as he'd done every morning. He sat down, had his breakfast, stood up and wiped the food off his mouth with the sleeve of his dingy shirt. He then wiped his hands on his pants, guzzled down the rest of his ale, and made his proclamation. She had been waiting for that announcement since she turned seventeen and yet did not hear it until today, three days after her eighteenth birthday. Likely because he had needed a nursemaid until now.

"Well, my girl, today's your lucky day. You're going to have a husband by nightfall. You are eighteen now, so it's high time that you get a husband. I'll make that my work for the day, and you'll be glad to know that I have been looking for a good one for you. While I don't think you'll bring in any type of money, I might be able to get a few pence for you. Possibly a gold sovereign or two; who knows? More likely, I'll get a good trade." He retrieved a key and tossed it to her. "Comb out your hair and look in that trunk in the corner. See if there's anything in there of your mother's that you want. But whatever you do, be quick about it, for I am determined that you'll spend the night under your husband's roof. I have asked around, and there are several interested if you would believe it."

With a crude attempt at a laugh, the man was gone from the room. It seemed quite unlikely that she would be able to get a husband today, but she knew he had spoken of it often, so she decided today was just as good a day as the next. She knew that this was a big market day, so possibly there would be a chance that she might find a man who wasn't as rude and crude as her stepfather. Rather like buying a chicken at the market. Her hopes weren't high, though, and she decided that if the choice were terrible, she would run away before going with him.

She had thought about running away most of the year, but where would she run to and for what purpose? She would end up the same way. She tried to stay for her little brother. She was the only mother he had, and she was reticent to remove that last female warmth from his life. Well, she had done what she could. Maybe she could bring him with her? But she knew that was a fairy dream. Her stepfather had plans for his son.

Happy to rummage through her mother's old things, few and scant though they were, she was hopeful she could possibly find some items that she would use in her new life. Her best friend's father had done this same thing to her just the other week. Just hours after she turned eighteen, the girl was out the door and living with another man who didn't even take her in matrimony.

That brought up another fear that Annalise always had. She feared that a man would take her to be with him for a short period of time, not forever. Oh, she had no illusions that men married women for love all the time. More often, in her situation, the men had no expectation of doing more than bedding, for their entertainment and affections were taken elsewhere. And if it were an advantageous union, of which she need not worry hers would be, the husband was just as likely to be cruel. Some alliances were simply in name only, not even taking his wife to bed.

Annalise never wanted to be that woman, the "elsewhere" woman, that men went to find entertainment. She would be perfectly happy and content if a man would take her to wife and all he wanted was children. She could actually make quite a content life that way. But if the man wanted to do more than reproduce, Annalise worried she didn't know how to be a good wife. She barely knew what a good husband was.

Annalise found a dress in the trunk and hastily put it on. She took one last look at herself in the glass and made one last shake of the dress that her mother had worn to church and only those most special of occasions and decided she looked just as good as she possibly could. She found a worn brush in her mother's trunk and used it to put some order into her hair. She set about gathering what few things she had that she could take with her today if indeed her stepfather bargained her away.

If she were to leave today, she decided she was not scrubbing floors or pots and pans, nor was she chasing after her half-brother. No, Annalise decided that today she was not cooking dinner for them only to hear their insults at her abilities, insults even her brother had begun to join her stepfather in saying. No, today she was going to be a lady of leisure, whatever that truly meant. For her, besides no chores, it meant spying to see the gentlemen who came in to purchase things from her stepfather to see if any of them seemed likely to walk away with more than the usual wares.

She slipped out of the back room just as her stepfather had begun to solicit those who he was doing business with to spread the word that he had a lovely young woman for a good trade or payment. A fresh and clean young girl. The implications were obvious, and it made Annalise blush. He made it known that today was the day she was to choose, but he was the one choosing based upon the best payment offered or trade given, and no one challenged the morality or legality of that statement. Something inside told her that shouldn't be right.

Annalise left her stepfather's gun shop next door as it was rather crowded due to her stepfather's trade of not-only-guns today. She had just stepped outside in time to watch as a grand coach pulled up. She then watched the very handsome gentleman who was bundled up in wool and what appeared to be cashmere quickly step into the leather shop next door. She loved the leather shop with its earthy scent and the feeling of well-being she always had when she was in there. Leather was comforting, unlike gunmetal, grease, and black powder.

There wasn't much that she could do at this point since her stepfather had made his declaration, but she could draw comfort in the little things that she had for today. And one of those little things was watching a very handsome lord walk into her favorite shop and imagine what it would be like to be with him.

Annalise was young, but she was wise beyond her years on some things. And she knew what she didn't have. She knew she didn't have security or someone who cared about her other than her half-brother, who was already learning to be stingy with his affection.

She thought of the loss of the merchants she had as neighbors. The tobacco vendor was a kindly man of foreign birth and had taught her all she needed to know about good leaves. He said it was part of a proper education for a girl who would someday be a wife. If she knew good tobacco, she would never buy less for her husband and men appreciated the attention to their comfort.

"Don't men buy their own pipe tobacco?" she had inquired.

He pooh-poohed her and offered to let her try some snuff. "Women of quality are known to indulge," he promised. She'd sneezed hard and had gotten a headache, but it cured her curiosity. It now comforted her to simply smell the finer tobacco rather than indulge.

The leather goods shopkeeper had never shooed her out in all the years that she had lived in the back of the gunsmith shop next door. It was almost as though he knew she needed unconditional love and acceptance from somewhere. His wife was very kind and had always done little things for Annalise, especially after her mother passed away.

She sighed as she decided to walk into the leather shop just to entertain her dreams a bit longer pretending, she was there with his lordship, seeking out her own items at his request. It was a game she often played in the leather shop. What would she buy if she had the money and what would she do with it when she bought it? That was the game and today could quite possibly be the last time she played it, so she would indulge.

As she slipped through the door and closed it quickly behind her to keep all the heat inside, she did as she always did. She took a slow, restorative breath, allowing the essence to permeate her very soul before she released her pent-up breath. She then opened her eyes, eagerly looking for the shopkeeper and his wife. When her sight fell upon the merchant, she smiled a genuine greeting. The response she received was not what she had expected. The owner returned her smile but in a sadly resigned way. He began to shoo her back out the door. *This must be a very important customer for him to not even allow me a moment of respite.*

She looked up just as several more gentlemen were entering the shop looking at a variety of hand-tooled and handwoven tack and leather. Her gaze traveled to the finely dressed gentleman she had followed in and met his eyes watching her. Annalise watched him boldly for a moment, and he sent a nod her way, causing her to stare another moment before she dropped her eyes.

Having the odd sensation of wanting to draw the gentleman's attention even more, she crossed her arms, as was her penchant when thwarted. She turned pouty lips and soulful eyes quickly on the gentleman before allowing them to meet the merchant's gaze. She gave the shopkeeper a pleading look and silently requested to be allowed to stay.

"Go along, Annalise. Your father has said you are to stay at the gunsmith's today."

"Stepfather," she snapped. If she were not to get her way, then she did not need to be civil. For a moment, there was quite a bit of resentment and hardness in her tone before she released the anger and changed her tune. "Oh please, may I stay?" she asked in a very polite but entreating way. Her face was still the picture of a pouting child. "He doesn't want me today. He doesn't want me any day. He's attempting to give me away today. Have you not heard?" The hardness seeping back into her voice was evident in her stance and tone.

The shopkeeper was having none of it. "Young lady, you do as I say. I'm only following what your stepfather has said, and regardless of how you feel about him, you must obey. Go along now before I get the strap."

Annalise stomped her foot and issued a disgruntled noise. "He is selling me to the highest bidder, you know. I would not say he is a man who one should esteem nor abide by his requests."

She looked over as her eyes met the handsome lord's eyes once again. She had forgotten he was even in the shop. She physically deflated when she watched the raising of his eyebrows on his determined face. He appeared to want to say something and indeed cleared his throat ominously and yet refrained. Annalise felt like a naughty little girl whose papa had discovered her disobedience, and yet she felt it was a righteous indignation.

Nonetheless, it was as though he were warning her of retribution and advising her not to make it worse by the movement of that brow. It made her suck her lower lip into her mouth and bite down with her teeth. Her tummy felt queasy, and her whole body heated up. There was a tingle in her lower belly that she had not had before.

She made one more thwarted sound of irritation and stomped one more time as she twirled quickly and opened the door wide, hoping all the warm air would slide out in her wake. She knew it was childish. Indeed, her whole display had been juvenile, but Annalise hadn't been a child for very long. She knew that when she was incensed and didn't get her way, she either swallowed it deep or occasionally resorted to her six-year-old behavior of which she was later embarrassed. Today, her mind must've opted for the young child, for she did not believe that she could swallow another dose of bile at all.

She had learned to stuff her emotions down most of her life. She swallowed the rejection, the disappointment, and the pain that she experienced. She'd learned to do that by living under the roof with a man who had no compassion and little empathy for anything but himself. It was certain he had none for her.

She didn't know why she felt that it was okay to behave in such a way as she did in front of the handsome man, but she did. Now she was thoroughly embarrassed. But more than that, she wondered why his look of disapproval excited her. A strange thought went through her mind. She wondered what it would be like to be chastised and then loved by that man. She could not identify the reason, but she felt she would always be safe with him. He would protect her.

She walked next door to the front of the gun shop and sat on a half barrel that she had placed a piece of wood across a long time ago, creating a bench. It was a convenient place to sit and watch the world go by, dreaming of what it would be like to be any one of them. And so today she was dreaming that she was going to belong to that handsome lord. The one who she felt confident would take her in hand if she belonged to him and had such a display of temper. She wondered what that would be like. To be loved so much by someone that they cared enough to take her to task.

Her mother had been so ill after having given birth to her brother Julian that all Annalise could do was help her without complaint. And then when the infection was severe, she took over the care of the baby and his father, her stepfather. Her mother had been so grateful, but soon the sickness overcame her, and she died. And the old goat, instead of having any type of compassion for a young girl of twelve who'd lost her mother after having lost her father, simply used her as a servant and nursemaid to his son.

But not anymore. Today was Annalise's day of freedom. Wherever that freedom took her, she would go. The noise inside the small shop was louder than usual with the extra men inside. Annalise thought about running away, contemplated it one more time before she booted it out of her mind completely. Of course, she told herself, she could always revisit that thought if the life that she was shuffled off to was anything less than biddable.

The cold was seeping inside her thin coat, the chill becoming more noticeable, and still she remained sitting outside. Annalise looked up as the leather shop door opened while trying to suppress an intense shiver. It was the handsome man. She resolved to put on her best manners and to behave like those ladies of quality who she had seen walk along the streets on their shopping adventures. She could imitate the haughty look as well and pretend that the gentleman was not even in her visual purview. That is what was expected of ladies of quality. Never acknowledge the gentlemen openly but if you did, do it with disdain.

The man turned in the direction of Annalise and paused before taking a step towards her. She panicked for a second, not sure what she should do. But then the man spoke in a deep, rich, commanding voice, knocking her completely off balance, and she came tumbling down from her mental perch. She frowned in her trepidation.

Chapter 3

Lord Thayer intended to attempt to strike up a conversation with that young lady. There was something about her that piqued his interest. He told himself part of it was the fact that she all but threw a full-blown tantrum right in the middle of the shop. Oh, not like a refined lady's outburst, but a stomping, squealing fit. She needed a spanking. Unfortunately, it wasn't his to give. However, he wished that it were. He could imagine gazing at her bared bottom, bringing his hand down on her silky pale cheek, turning it pink. She would squirm and wiggle and probably cry out, but he'd slap the other cheek, turning it a matching pink. His cock jumped just thinking about accomplishing that task. His cock hadn't stirred in a long time.

She really was a beauty. Her golden blonde hair, while not totally clean, still shined and called for his fingers to run through the strands. He envisioned washing her hair and watching it dry to glorious strands of honey. He'd caught the smile that she had been displaying as she walked into the leather shop before it was wiped totally away by the keeper. He wondered what it would be like for her to shine her smile on him, happy to see him.

Her skin was fair, her eyes were a sparkling bright blue, and her cheeks held two brilliantly bright spots of red, in angry protest of the cold that they endured. She looked like a little China doll. A China doll he wanted to dress up and cuddle as a papa should. He spoke, hoping to tease a bit more from her disheartened face and full, downturned lips. He envisioned those ample lips around his cock.

"My dear, it is too cold to be outside in that paltry cloak in these elements, with no task to complete. The idleness will freeze you."

Annalise twisted around and said, "Oh, no, my lord. I am much safer out here than inside, where my stepfather is auctioning me off to the highest bidder."

He laughed. "My dear, you are surely too young to marry. And no reasonably sane man would do that to his daughter."

"Then you have fallen upon the reason. My stepfather is an insane person. And I am not too young, I can assure you. If there is to be a marriage proposal transacted at the end of this day I know not, but it is certain that I will leave this place with a man today, but it is not certain that I am to be married."

"What?"

"My *step*-father has said as I am eighteen and have no prospects, he will give me to the highest bidder. I am to be sold, in harsher terms."

"That is not allowable."

"Well, the whole of England does it, my lord. I am sure you did so for your wife. Men pay a debt called a dowry, and it is to secure a suitable placement for their daughters. So, in essence, money is exchanged for a bribe, for making a good marriage. Only, in this case, the codger inside is *taking* money rather than giving it. Selling me. It is just not seen as polite to name it as such, but a transaction for money in exchange for product, nonetheless."

Stephen chuckled at the impertinence of the little hoyden but tried to camouflage his indiscretion with a cough. "Yes, well, it is unladylike to point it out, however."

"True, but I believe in naming things as they are, so there are no misunderstandings. Do you not think it is ungentlemanly to engage in such a transaction?"

"Yes, well, nonetheless, you must go inside now." His voice deepened to accentuate his expectation of compliance.

Annalise turned her sparkling blue eyes toward Stephen beseechingly. "Truly, must I? I am not in the mood to go in as of yet. Might I please stay out here a little longer?"

Stephen gazed into her eyes, surprised at her response. He found himself disappointed at the docile reply and yet tantalized at the same time. She vacillated from sassy young lady, to a little one who needed her arse smacked. He wanted to pull himself up from her blue depths and take her home with him at that very moment, but he needed to find out what she was playing at. She was such a sprite and one he would love to learn more about, but he needed to be firm. It was entirely too cold. And surely her Banbury tale should be addressed.

He did marvel at his manhood that began to make itself known regardless of the weather, and it simply wouldn't do. She was a slender lass, young but not as naïve as one might have expected, and yet her immaturity and inexperience showed through. In fact, upon closer examination, he was sure she had not met her majority. Did he care? Shamefully not.

Even with that expectation, he knew it was she who he had been looking for, this woman/child. She was sparkling and enchanting, a maiden and yet a woman of understanding. Her intelligence was quite noticeable, and if she were of the upper classes, she would have been labeled a bluestocking, for she would have access to all manner of knowledge and he had no doubt that she would have absorbed it. But she wasn't of his class or even close. The merchant class was not expected to marry into the aristocracy and certainly he was not to offer her that grand step up. He had a duty to his family and yet he ached when he thought of her living with another. He thought to try an experiment.

He hardened his voice slightly as he had just done and watched her reaction. "Yes, it is time to go inside, my dear. Up you go." He took a step towards her and watched her stand quickly in response and take a step back. "No, no, young lady. Time to go inside, or you'll catch your death."

Her eyes flashed. "Well, I won't. I've no reason to abide by your words." Stephen stifled a smile once again. Yes, while her words were resistant, her tone was hesitant and yet petulant. Her face was a bit pouty, and yet her stance was stubborn. Lovely.

"What is your name, young lady?" His pitch did not change from the reprimanding tone and he watched her response.

She hesitated for a moment and then answered. "Annalise Coton. If you intend on bringing my stepfather into the fray, you need not bother. He could not care less if I freeze, but then he might get less for me."

"That is a horrid thing to say."

Stephen was appalled at the assumption, however, he was none too sure that she wasn't speaking the truth. He would need to go in and observe this man for himself as soon as he got her into the warmth. He rather expected that everything she had been saying could be poppycock and balderdash, and he was a man to go to the source for the information. He intended to heat her bottom cheeks if she were weaving him a Banbury tale.

"Even if there is truth in it?" Her words were delivered quietly, and she shivered with the cold she was refusing to come in from.

He softened his manner and spoke gently. "Yes, little one. You need to learn to curb your tongue."

"Or aim it better." She mumbled the words but screeched her dismay at the solid swipe he made to her upper thighs with his walking stick. "I thought those were for show," she cried out with both hands reaching for her bitten legs.

Even though she had on a cloak, it was too short and the dress too thin for the season. It was no protection from the cold or his cane. The swipe was intentionally hard, landing on her predominately unprotected limbs.

"And now you know they are not."

Stephen watched her as she rubbed her stinging thighs. He was thinking things he knew he should not as he watched her massage the smarting bite the cane had left her. She wiped the errant tear from her face. He wanted to dry her tears. His thoughts were of cuddling her after chastisement, and he did not have the right. Yet. He almost smothered the smile successfully, but just a twinge touched his lips, and it was not missed by the sweet morsel in front of him.

She was a proud bit of fluff, and he could see her struggle to avoid being entertainment for anyone, especially him. The man that just slapped her legs with his cane and caused her grief. He watched her face grimace as though she hated to give up her self-comforting. She shivered almost violently. He watched her very resolutely stop mid rub and sit down, arms folded across her bosom, but she was unable to forestall the little wiggle to more gently settle onto the wood plank.

"Come on, young lady, I am out of patience, and you are freezing. Let us go inside." He put his arm out to usher her inside, and she turned her head away.

It was evident that she was beginning to feel the chill quite profoundly, and he needed to get his little sprite inside, but at this moment she needed to maintain her stance, thereby retaining her dignity. He knew she would try to stay outside. While Stephen was not accustomed to having his word challenged or ignored, he could see her glee at doing just that. Defy him to his face regardless of, or because of, his chastisement. He didn't know. But he was not playing any longer; she indeed would catch her death out here so lightly dressed. As he opened his mouth to end the game, she spoke.

"If you please, go inside, but I am pleased to stay here. I'll not go in there whilst I am the most bartered piece of property in that shop today." Her demeanor changed to one of pleading, as he had seen inside the leather shop. "Besides, they are not kind men, I can assure you, my lord. I am, by far, safer here."

He was furious that she was so cold that she was unable to control the shiver that overcame her when a cold wind blew past, and yet she chose to remain out of doors. He was angry that any man could treat a young woman like a piece of chattel. This sweetheart was more than a chattel. Well, she wasn't his sprite yet, but he was determined to have her.

Stephen clapped his hands together to ward off the cold and said ominously, "Suit yourself, but I will not forget the insolence, just you beware, my little sprite."

"I'm full grown. I am nobody's little sprite," and yet she sighed when he ran his gloved hand over her cheek, leaning slightly into it. She raised her big blue eyes that held a message of the lost, yet hopeful.

Encouraged by her look, he thought that maybe that he would take her in hand. That he would make her mind his words. That he would protect her. That he would make her his, as she seemed to be asking. He dropped to his haunches, taking her cold hands into his, and placed his lips on each palm before looking up into her face.

"Not yet maybe, but you soon will be. Come in with me, Annalise."

Tears tumbled down her cheeks. "Please don't make me. I can't bear it. Please, my lord, may I go into the tobacco shop instead?"

Chapter 4

If she could go to the back of the shop and slide in the window without him seeing her leave her appointed perch, she would. She was frightfully cold and would be ill soon if she did not go back inside. She wanted to win the standoff, and yet she was losing the battle to the weather. She fleetingly revisited the pipe dream of belonging to him. She didn't even get his name, but when he nodded his assent that she go into the tobacco shop, she smiled. She had won the standoff and yet she hadn't, for he refused to move until he saw her enter inside. She looked back out, and he was gone.

The tobacco shop owner was busy, so she sat in the shop for a few moments thinking of his lordship. He would be stern and strict. She had no doubts about that, but he would take perfect care of her. He showed he could be gentle and, dare she say, loving. She would not want for anything, discipline or coddling. But he struck with his cane, and she had been so cold that at first, she did not feel the attack. Within seconds, the offensive line of pain streaked across her legs, its fire reverberating through her body. Yes, he would be that type of man. The spanking kind. And her belly flipped as she cried out.

Her stepfather had struck her several times quite nastily, but one could not have confused it with a thrashing. He had cuffed her along the side of her head and had slapped her quite frequently, but her perception of who this lord, her lord, was would never allow that. Nor would he ever engage in such activity. Slapping was a personal attack. Somehow, spanking was not. It was a correction by someone who cared.

Not that she had actually ever remembered more than one real spanking. It was given by her father when she was young. She did not even remember the infraction or much of the spanking, but it was the cuddling afterward that stayed in her memory. It was one of her most vivid memories of her father. One she cherished.

This man would thrash thoroughly but would he also cuddle? She wanted to believe so. And here she was in her pretend world expecting that if she had not gone in, he would have put paid to her sitting ability. But in reality, he had left. It had been such a children's game she played, but there it was. It was over now. She wondered who remained inside the gun shop and were they there to barter for her.

Her thoughts ran to concern as she worried what her life would truly be like after today. While the existence she presently had was not wonderful, it was comfortable in its predictability. Her mind wandered back to the gentleman who spoke to her and to whom she was cheeky. He would be nice to work for realistically and, in her dreams, marry.

Well, it didn't look as though the fine gentleman was coming back and this shop was kept cooler than the gun shop. She needed to warm up her still numb body, so she left the tobacco merchant still busy. She went inside the darker, dingier shop full of dirty, sweaty bodies, grease, and gunpowder. She loved the smell of leather in the shop next door but liked nothing about the smell of gunmetal, oil, and powder in her stepfather's shop.

Today there was also the scent of expensive tobacco and soap, which she enjoyed, but the rest made her almost gag. She was used to the smell, but something made it extra pungent today. Probably the odor of greed from her stepfather and the scent of lecherous men who were after her innocence at the lowest price possible.

As she walked into the shop, a man reached out and grabbed her wrist, and before she knew it, he was trying to shove his finger into her mouth. She screeched in outrage and bit down on his digit, which brought a slap across her face for her trouble.

"Just checking the wares. I might be the one to give your step-father enough blunt to take ye home, gel. Better be careful to mind your manners. The more the distaste of the merchandise, the lower the price." He laughed, a tainted, rough cackle delivered on foul breath.

"If he sold me to you, I would run and drown myself in the river."

The man wheezed, "At least ye'd be clean." The surrounding males laughed as well.

She cringed and wrenched herself away from the group of men and walked over to the corner where the coal stove sat and put her hands near its heat stopping to rub her now aching cheek. One of the men there placed his grubby hands on her breast and squeezed hard. She yelped loudly in pain. Angrily, she lambasted him with words he would have had to go to the docks to hear, and she delivered them with all sincerity. The man laughed and yanked her hair hard.

"You need to get used to those touches, girl. I mean to take you home at the close of business today." Scared but angrier, she stomped her worn shoe's heel into his instep and listened to the howl with a satisfaction she seldom felt.

"I would rather die first, you—" A hand was placed over her mouth that was neither dirty nor invasive. It smelled of tobacco, but it was over her mouth firmly.

She fought, twisting her body as the other beasts laughed at the sight. In her ear was someone's hot breath and the faintest of sounds that she needed to stop her fight to hear. She smelled soap and some-thing else, but its mere presence bade her relax and listen to the qui-etly spoken words.

"Shh, my little sprite. Don't worry, I will handle this. You must agree to do as I say. Yes?" Annalise nodded her head, and he removed his hand.

Still speaking in her ear, he said, "Walk to the back and gather the things that you will keep and wait until you are called to go. Do not come back outside of your rooms until that time. Will you do that?" Annalise hesitated. "Promise me," he demanded harsher.

Annalise nodded, feeling the warmth of his heavily cloaked body against her cold frame, and shuffled a little closer. She looked into his eyes. Dark blue eyes met her gaze. She was sure that he was telling the truth, whatever that truth was, in the cryptic instructions. True blue was never more apparent in meaning than looking into this man's eyes and hearing his truth. He let go of her and stood back, nodding in the direction of the rooms in the back. Once he saw her answering nod, he waited until she made it to the dividing curtain. She looked back and saw he had turned and without so much as a backward glance, he walked out of the shop door.

There was left no misunderstanding that he expected to be obeyed once she agreed. He trusted her word. Even before she made it to the back rooms where they lived, she heard the carriage drive away, and the tears of her veritable predicament began to fall. This was no game that children played. This was horrifically real. She had to believe that this man would be as good as his word. He would take care of this. She saw the anger in his face and she knew it was not directed at her, but her maulers. The men who thought her nothing but property.

In the back room, she wanted to touch her breast, that was throbbing from the beastly assault on her now bruised tissue. She wanted to erase the memory of those filthy fingers from her person. She was able to gently massage some of the agonizing burn away before turning to gather her items, as the gentleman had instructed.

She wondered why she bothered because she'd heard him drive away. She sat and waited. It had been several hours since he had left and still nothing. He had no more use for her than the animals bartering for her in the front of the shop. However, she did indeed gather her meager belongings and placed them in the small satchel that had carried her worldly belongings into this place nearly eight years ago. She sat there for quite a spell and decided the gentleman didn't intend to take care of anything. Whatever it was she thought he would take care of, that is. He had obviously changed his mind. He did extricate her from the sordid predicament she had found herself in, and for that, she was thankful. The rest, her silly pipe dreams, were just that, smoke in the wind.

There was an uproar in the front of the shop and Annalise was sorely tempted to go out there to see what the commotion was about, but she didn't. Her lordship had told her to not come out until she was called for and she had not been called. The loud talking and irreverent banter was quiet now. There was the opening and closing of the door. Then silence.

It had been more than three hours since his lordship had left. She looked up to see the boy, who was her half-brother, as he ambled into the room. "Father said you were to come to him. He has someplace for you to go. Can I go with you? Will you have sweets?"

He had come back for her. The tears gathered in her eyes as she kissed the dirty child on the cheek, too much like his father already and said, "Not today, Jules, not today. When I come back, I will bring you sweets." He nodded as she left the room to enter into her fate.

Annalise carried her small valise over her shoulder and walked into the shop with her head held high, her lower lip in her teeth. She walked into a room occupied by her stepfather and one additional person. A man she had not met before, nor had she seen him come into the shop previously. But then again, so many had come in today. Most ventured a look out of curiosity, some out of interest, apparently only one to make a final deal. It came as no surprise to her that she did not recognize him. He looked rather expectantly at her and, after a few seconds, cocked his head to the left.

"Are you Annalise Coton?" he asked, as if he was not sure.

"Yes," she answered, her curiosity peaked. "Who are you?"

"I am the man who has paid your dowry price, and I have come to take you back with me. But tell me before we go if this man has the right to consent to your choice?" Annalise looked confused. "The name, it is different."

"She is my stepdaughter. Of course, I have the right." The gentleman ignored Charles Hayfield and looked at Annalise to confirm. She nodded her head. He nodded in understanding. "As I was saying, I paid your bride price, and you are free to come with me."

"And a fine price it was. I didn't think to get quite this much for you, but it will be enough for the trouble." Her stepfather came from the back storage room, looking rather pleased with himself.

She ignored the man who would speak of selling her without any remorse or delicacy and concentrated on the dowry payer. He was rather clean and his clothes were well mended. He was not a lord or even of Gaston, but he seemed to possibly work for them. It would not be a bad life if her husband were to work for a lord or squire because they would have a roof over their head and plenty to eat. He sounded kind.

"And what do you do, sir?"

"Me? Oh, I'm no sir, I'm just Reggie." He wiped his hands on his coat and put out one hand awkwardly. "Reginald Tate. I keep his lordship's stables."

He seemed suddenly out of place and ill at ease, so she said, "Are we going to my new home, Reggie?"

"Oh, yes. We are-I mean, it is time for us to go right after you help me with picking the right saddle for his lordship's fiancée. As a woman, I imagine you to know what the best choice is. Are you ready?"

And with no more than a mere tilt of the head, she left her home of eight years with the only remorse the loss of her brother in her daily life. She felt confident she would see him again, but did worry about his future under the influence of his father. She continued out the door to walk with Reggie to the leather and tack shop.

"Is money an object of consideration, Reggie?" she asked as they walked to the saddles. She had had her eye on a beauty, and in her fairy world, she was able to simply walk in and purchase it. There were some ready for sale if waiting or personal tooling was not desired. She, of course, knew what tooling she would have on it, but would have wanted to do that herself, as the shopkeeper had taught her. Perhaps his lordship's fiancée would also do her own hand tooling.

"No. And I imagine his lady to sit a horse about like you would sit."

"Oh, well, then that makes this choice quite easy. This is the best sidesaddle. Now, if his lordship's fiancée wanted to be more daring and sit more comfortably, then she would take this saddle and sit astride." She knew she was being impertinent but was surprised when Reggie appeared to consider it.

"Well, if you had a choice, which seat would you choose?"

"Oh, the saddle that sits astride. But it isn't for me, so I am sure the only appropriate one would be this sidesaddle."

She wondered what this morning's gentleman would have said if she rode astride instead of sidesaddle as a lady was expected to travel. She clenched her bottom cheeks, as she was quite sure what his response would be. She wished she could try that premise out.

But she was to go to her new home now, as a stray dog taken in due to sympathy or pity. She should be thankful for whatever it was that came her way, but she simply had a hard time doing it. She found it difficult to not feel sorry for her loss of choices. Scolding herself, she resolutely put that out of her mind and went into her new life with the expectation of happiness in whatever form it came. Reggie seemed like an honorable man, if rather a lot older than she.

Having the side saddle put on his lordship's account, he guided her out of the shop while carrying the impressive bit of leather out to the open work wagon. He helped her to sit on the bench with him, and she wondered how far they would need to go as the weather had not let up, and she would be cold through and through before too long.

Reggie slapped the reins of the sturdy work geldings and started the wagon rolling. Annalise sat quite still, careful not to move and lose any of her heat, for she still did not know how far they would go.

When she asked Reggie, he only said, "Just down the road apiece."

Which of course helped not at all, and since he wasn't inclined to fill in any further information, she felt disinclined to ask more questions. Just as they cleared the small village and were out on the main road, Annalise thought to ask a more defined question.

"And which lord do you work for, Reggie?"

"Lord Stephen Thayer, the gentleman whom I believe you were speaking to here earlier."

"At least I know his name now. And since you work for him, Reggie, well, that answers another question."

"And what question was that?"

"Well, it answers the question that I had as to what his lordship meant when he said he would take care of everything. So I don't know how much you had to bargain and pay for me, Reggie, but now I know his lordship made it so that I wouldn't have to go with one of those mangy curs." She turned and looked at Reggie for a few moments, as though contemplating her next words.

"Had you intended to buy a wife today, Reggie? Or indeed had you expected to take a wife at all in the near future?" She looked at him with quiet curiosity and watched as his face turned quite red from either embarrassment or anger as well as cold. She didn't know which. He didn't look at her, choosing instead to concentrate on driving the wagon.

"No, my missus might not be happy about that." He laughed. "But I don't believe you understand completely. You are to go to the main house, the manor."

Reggie seemed to believe that's all that needed to be said to fill in any other blank she might have. All it did, in fact, was present more questions.

"And what is it exactly that I am to do in the manor, Reggie?" Her teeth chattered.

"Oh, miss, I was to give you this cloak to wear. He was most specific and here I've forgotten and you are nearly frozen to death. I am so sorry." He produced a cloak she was well familiar with. It was his Lordship's. He must be freezing himself, but she gratefully accepted the warmth it provided. The scent of his lordship, clean and crisp, surrounded her in comfort and peace.

Annalise held her breath for the answer that he could supply, for she couldn't imagine what it was that she would do in a grand manor. She was sturdy, and of a comfortable height, it was true, but her frame was petite. It would've been referred to as delicate if she were of the Gaston and not a shopkeeper's daughter.

Nevertheless, she'd pulled her weight for the last eight years, and she could continue to do so. In fact, it was a bit freeing to know she could live independently of her stepfather without having to take a husband. It wasn't that she would not want one eventually, but being quite young herself afforded her a little bit of time to look.

While Annalise had been thinking, it was apparent that Reggie had been thinking as well. "Did you think that I would take you to wife? You could be my daughter. T'wouldn't be right."

"Well, you can't fault my logic. You were the gentleman in the shop. You did announce that you had just paid the bride price and did not disabuse me of the natural conclusion."

"Because I knew that I was paying for another. It never crossed my mind that you would think that I was to be your husband. Now that you say it, it does make quite a bit of sense, but I assure you I will not be that man."

"Of course. You have a wife. Besides, a man wants a woman he has courted. Not a young girl as myself." But the way she said it told of her lack of understanding and lack of self-confidence.

"I would have taken you if it were in my power to do so, my dear. And if Mrs. Tate wouldn't have my head. You seem to be well mannered and of a content nature."

Annalise laughed, her first of the day. "Oh, I am flattered and quite sure you would have. I am convinced I would have thought it lovely." She replied without the confidence of the truth of the words.

Reggie slowed the wagon down and looked up ahead. There were several carriages parked along the way and several horses tied to the side of what appeared to be a roadhouse. A pub for travelers and, she had no doubt for the local people. She was already further from the shop than she had been since arriving there. The Ale and Chop seemed quite full for this time of day.

She turned over to Reggie and asked, "Why are we here? Are we so far away from his lordship's property that we have need to stay here?" The cold having sheared through to her bones, she gave a shiver and her teeth chattered, but she pretended to not notice since she was now wrapped in the cloak but it had done very little to help her warm. It would take a great deal of time for her to feel thawed.

"Oh no, I was merely instructed to bring you here. You need to get inside, miss, you are freezing near to death. It won't do, it won't do at all."

"I am hardier than that. For what purpose am I here?"

Annalise was beginning to feel some anxiety as to possibly what the true state of her existence may be. Surely they wouldn't hire her out to be a serving wench? It was apparent Reggie had no other information and blithely followed the instructions he was given without any concern. She was so cold her mind was numb, causing her thinking to slow.

Annalise knew serving was something she could do, except she didn't agree to it. In fact, she had, hadn't she? She had listened to his lordship and when he instructed her to do something she did not question, she simply did it. Just as Reggie had done. As she now questioned her own sanity, she began to shake continually. She was freezing.

How ludicrous and stupid to listen to a man you never met before and had no idea of his credentials and then do whatever he said. And now she would freeze to death because she needed to get away from these people who thought they could order her about without recourse or so much as a by your leave.

Reggie had already jumped down from the wagon and was putting his hands up to help Annalise down from her perch. "His lordship will be angry if you become ill from the cold. He'd be taking his crop after me if anything were to happen to you, miss."

She didn't understand what he meant exactly but appreciated his manner towards her, and she graced him with an enormous frozen grin. Now that she knew he was not to be her husband, she relaxed in his company and felt him to be someone she could count on as her friend. After all, were they not both to be employed by the same person?

"I th-thank you, Reggggie. It is mo-most kind of you to help me." She attempted to show manners she was never called on to use since before her mother's death.

"You're quite welcome, my lady." He said it so naturally, she pretended for just a short time that it was something that all people would address her as, my lady. She allowed him to lead her into The Ale and Chop for whatever future awaited her there.

"Oh wait, don't I need my satchel?" Annalise turned to grab her bag and was stayed by Reggie.

"Oh, don't worry about that, my lady. When you're ready for it, I will get it for you." He dismissed her concern easily.

"Yes, but won't you be gone as soon as I enter?" Annalise still didn't understand.

"Don't worry, when you need it, you will have it. I wouldn't keep your valuables from you."

"But—" Reggie's step picked up momentum, and it appeared as though he was impatient to drop her off. He, therefore, had no intentions of answering any further questions, adding to Annalise's confusion.

As they walked into the inn, the sound was quite loud with laughter and frivolity. The room was blessedly warm and then almost hot compared to her body. It was a bit early for the evening meal, but she supposed if you were done for the day, then it was time to eat. And for many single men who had no wife to cook for them, coming to a pub to eat was relatively normal. Her own belly rumbled at the smells of stew. She hadn't eaten enough today.

She tripped over her borrowed cloak and gathered the lengths in her hand. She began to change her thinking as to her fate bringing her here. She looked around and thought it was a clean place, and the men did not appear to be very handsy with the serving girls, so it might not be such a bad place to work. Her concern was where she was to stay if there were no quarters for the employees. She thought that could be worked out relatively easy. She hoped.

As she waited for Reggie to bring her over to the owner, to introduce his newest employee, she was surprised when he went in the opposite direction of the bar counter, over to a far corner of the pub. As she approached, she saw the back of a well-groomed head that seemed a bit out of place amongst the ordinary workers. There was something rather familiar about that head, but she could not place why. As Reggie brought her up closer to where the gentleman was sitting, Reggie called out to him.

"Here she is, your lordship. I did just as you asked. I paid the price you told me to. She picked out the saddle, and we came here. Is there anything else that you would have me do before I go back to the stables?"

"No, you've done well, Reggie, thank you. Here, have my seat, stay and have some dinner. I think Miss Coton and I are needed upstairs in the front parlor."

He tossed the payment for Reggie's meal on the table and took Annalise with him. She had wished to sit down with Reggie and have a meal, for she had only a piece of bread and some ale that morning. But it was not to be as she was led away. His lordship tucking her arm into his and her other hand holding up the voluminous amount of cloth from his cloak. She wondered what all of this was about as she fought the shivering of her still frozen body. Not one to wait too long for her answers, she simply blurted out the questions.

"What is going on and what are we doing here? And what am I doing with you?" There was no response. "Am I to work for you or not? I am confident to assume you are the lordship Reggie was talking about? That he works for?" She waited a few seconds before charging onward. "Or have you loaned me out to this place?"

She threw her free arm across the air in front of her. She tripped over the cloak and saw it whipped from her body and thrown over his other arm. She changed her tactic and adjusted her delivery to match a more refined woman in hopes of gaining a response. "And whatever it is, if you would be so kind as to disclose, I would be most appreciative."

And at just that moment, she shivered, for even though she had worn his cloak for a short period of time and the pub was warm, and she felt the warmth of his lordship's body, she could not get warm enough.

"What's wrong? Are you frightened, my little sprite?"

"No, my lord, cold. I apologize."

"What? Still cold from this morning?"

"No, sir, cold from the ride." She suppressed another tremor.

"But you had my cloak."

She didn't want to get Reggie in trouble, so she said nothing. He had turned them towards a small room but stopped mid-step and immediately redirected her to the massive fireplace in the grand room next to them, grabbing a chair to sit in and placing her in his lap.

"My lord," she whispered, "this is improper."

"Nonsense. I will tell you what is improper."

"But my lord—"

"Do not, little one, do not say it. Warm up. We have things yet to do today."

"But..." She felt him roll her into his broad chest and then the searing pain of the slap he left on her thigh. "Ow, may I not even speak?"

"Not when you are disobedient in that speech. Hush now and let the fire warm you."

She rubbed her thigh and whimpered as she cuddled into his broad chest unconsciously.

She almost fell asleep but wasn't allowed when Stephen murmured in her ear.

"We need to get up, my little sprite. One more big thing to do today. Up, Annalise."

Groggily she arose from his lap with Stephen's help, and as her mind came back to her predicament, her curiosity took over.

"What is it we must do, my lord?"

His lordship simply reached over and patted her hand, not even sparing her a glance. He kept his eyes forward and led her to what was obviously a front parlor. Standing in the room was another gentleman to which it was obvious even to Annalise that he was a minister.

"You've given me to a minister, or have you loaned or sold me to him? You can't meet me, pay my price, then have someone just bring me to some place, this place and then offer me to the first man who needs a woman." She jerked her arm out from his and stood with her arms akimbo, in a stance of anger. She had fallen for his tenderness as he led her to the slaughter. More fool her. She stamped her foot to add an exclamation to her point.

Lord Thayer laughed. He had the audacity to engage in a belly laugh full of gaiety while she stood there without means of understanding her situation. And that was funny? It was then that she noticed that the minister was quite flustered and was rearranging his collar as though there was not enough room for it to stay in position comfortably. What had she missed? What was wrong here besides the obvious?

"Oh, Reverend, I mean you no disrespect. It is this man I feel disrespect for. He bought me and now he is trying to foist me on another. I didn't ask him to pay the price for me. I know you would not condone marrying a woman under those conditions. That is no way to acquire a wife. I am sure you must agree."

The minister was quite dazed at the disclosure and cleared his throat in righteous indignation.

"Lord Thayer, is what this young lady is proclaiming in any way a part of the truth?"

"It is a part of the truth, according to Miss Coton. It, however, is not the whole truth. Suffice it to say that she was in a dilemma that I was fortunate enough to be made aware of before it was too late. I, therefore, had my employee barter a deal with her father." He raised his finger just as Annalise was going to correct him and corrected his own statement. "Her stepfather, and I procured a way for her to have a better life. With me." Stephen stared at Annalise. "Splendid, my dear. I had expected a grand explosion. You have surprised me with your silence."

Annalise was irritated. "I am very glad that I am something to entertain you, sir. I, however, am not amused." She closed her mouth tightly.

"Annalise." He strengthened his voice as he repeated, "Annalise." At the change in tone, she turned to look at the minister and then back again at Lord Thayer.

"My lord, I still don't know what it is you desire of me. Am I to marry another, work in this establishment, work at your home, or something else? Your jester maybe?" Her tartness seemed to get his attention.

"That is enough, Annalise. Have you not been listening to me at all?" He cocked his head for just a moment and stared at her, waiting. "My dear, I intend to marry you myself."

Chapter 5

"Lord Thayer," the minister said, "surely you have not thought this through. She is not appropriate, my lord. She is a simple merchant's daughter."

"Stepdaughter," Stephen and Annalise corrected the poor clergyman simultaneously. Annalise felt warm inside that Lord Thayer would rectify the mistake on her behalf, but not enough to dismiss the way he was orchestrating things.

"I don't even know if she's of the age of majority, for she doesn't look old enough to marry. And, my lord, did you indeed barter for her?"

"Her stepfather was selling her to the highest bidder. I simply became that person. And as to her age, Annalise has informed me herself of her age without any knowledge of my plan or my thoughts. Indeed, I had no thoughts at that point except that she was a delightful child and at her declaration of majority age, I decided she would be mine. Must be mine."

The minister looked over at Annalise, who appeared taken aback by the remarks of Lord Thayer and the conversation between the men. "My dear, are you of the age of majority?"

"If you are asking me if I am twenty-one, the answer is obviously no. If you are asking me if I am eighteen and of an age that my stepfather could dispose of me, the answer is yes. And were you to ask me if I were thoroughly appalled at the way all of these men are treating me as though I were a piece of merchandise or cattle for the slaughter? Then the answer is also yes. Am I to have no say?"

"Ah," said the minister. It appeared to be all he intended to say on the issue except, "Shall we begin, my lord?"

Annalise stomped her foot again, put her fists on her hips, and let out a frustrated and angry shriek. When she saw that it brought a frown to Lord Thayer's face, she did it again. He calmly grabbed her upper arm and pulled her to him, leaning into her ear, allowing for her to hear his words clearly. While she was quite sure the minister could hear him, he put his body between her and the minister. The gesture of privacy was vaguely appreciated until he spoke.

"You may not stomp your foot, you may not shriek at me, nor may you, in any way, behave in an unladylike fashion. Please understand that your options are these. You can be left here to find employment as you may, be brought back to my home and given a servant's job there, go back to your stepfather's home to be re-bartered tomorrow, or accept my discipline and marry me. I would like to think there is no need for contemplation. However, if you believe there are better choices for you, please enlighten me." It was evident by the end of his declaration that Lord Thayer was not happy.

Annalise cursed her shaky and uncertain voice as she began to answer him.

"You know, of course, that I cannot go back to my stepfather's, and I don't wish to stay here, my lord." As she was speaking, she became less and less demanding in her tone and body language and more compliant. "And, my lord, I could work in your home. However, I don't know what I would be good at as I've never done that before, but I could learn. So if you don't mind, and if you promise not to be cruel, I would very much like to learn to be your wife."

"And accept my discipline."

SHE STOMPED HER FOOT at him again, and it was clear that some of her submission was leaving her. "What? What do you mean except your discipline?"

"Surely you are familiar with the word."

"The word? Of course, I understand the word. I don't understand your meaning of the word in context to me. What does it mean when you say it to me?" Annalise's eyes were flashing, and against his better judgment, it excited him to see her fire. He had no intention of allowing her to do anything except marry him, but to give her the illusion of choice would help her be more agreeable. He hoped. It obviously stirred his cock as well, for it began to dance under its covering, rendering the cloth to be less than adequate in disguising his male reaction to her female display.

He leaned down to speak even closer to her ear so as not to embarrass her, for it was not at all his desire to make her any more uncomfortable than he was sure she already was.

"A spanking would be typical and today, to accept my proposal that you become Lady Thayer, you must submit to my hand on your arse before we take our vows. And you must accept that while I pray it won't happen often, discipline is necessary in my home, and for my wife, it will include spankings."

"And what else?" she demanded.

Stephen hesitated for a moment. Ultimately he decided the need to have the conversation so he would have her explicit consent. If she agreed, he needed to lay his hand to her pretty little arse so that they could complete this joining before either one of them thought too hard about it. Although Stephen was quite sure he wouldn't back out, he was not at all sure Annalise wouldn't. He looked over at the minister and studied him for a moment.

"Might you give us a moment so that we could have a private discussion? Annalise feels it is important we speak first."

Stephen turned away from the minister as though he had no doubt that he would excuse himself from the room without another comment and wait to be requested entry again. That was the arrogance born of the aristocracy. He made no apology. It was that same ability that allowed him to manage his vast estate and those dependent on it, with great success.

He turned to the lovely young woman in front of him. "What other means of discipline might be employed?" he asked. Annalise nodded her head, her eyes wide. "For a sprite with an unruly mouth, I understand soap to be quite effective in taming it." Annalise opened her lips to speak, but Stephen held his hand up to stay her tongue.

"Let me finish, my dear, and then you may ask your question. There might be times when I am working at my desk or reading while you spend some quiet time in the corner thinking upon unwise choices. Obviously, there will be spankings for my blonde-haired sprite if she chooses to be defiant. It would probably suffice unless the infraction was significant, such as lying. That would certainly see something stronger."

"But, my lord, that is for children, and I am a grown woman."

"Yes, you are. But you will also be my wife, and I intend to discipline my wife if she needs it. And while you are definitely a young woman, I sense there is still a little girl who didn't get everything she needed at the appropriate time, and I would hope to be able to fill those needs as they are presented. Cuddling for one. These are things we will discuss later. But for now we need to get the ceremony complete and to do that, you must accept my proposal and my discipline first. I assure you, the vicar has many other things he could be doing, so we must be conscious of the time we are taking."

Annalise looked up into Lord Thayer's face. He reached his hand out and caressed her cheek. "Please, my dear. I am confident we will do well together. And I will cherish you and take care of you. On my honor, I shall protect you until my dying day."

"All right, my lord. I accept your proposal and your discipline. But why do I need to be disciplined now?"

Stephen smiled. "My dear, you've been quite naughty today. Disobeying when I instructed you to go inside. Staying outside until you were quite frozen, endangering your health. You put yourself in harm's way by sitting and watching the men coming in and out of the shop."

"But I told you about them."

"That you did, but you should have never taken up your perch in their direct path. And after I sent you to the tobacco merchant, you wandered back into the front of the gun shop knowing full well there were unsavory sorts inside. And I know you to understand that to place yourself in danger is inappropriate behavior. We should be quick about it." As Stephen reached for Annalise, she stepped back and withdrew her arm from his grasp.

"But it doesn't seem fair that you would hold me accountable for something I could not have been aware of at the time. I had no idea who you were, or that you would be my husband. And it's simply not done between a man and a woman before they are properly wed."

"I am not asking to bed you, just spank you. And I do see your point. However, I also know you knew it to be cheeky because I had already striped you once with the cane."

"But you don't intend to do that now, surely." Annalise made one more step backward, and she threw her hands behind her in the protection of her bottom.

Stephen saw that there was fear beginning to rise up in Annalise, and that was not his intention at all. He changed his tactics just slightly. His voice gentled and reasoned with her.

"Then let us do it this way. Let's not consider this discipline for anything that happened prior to our wedding. Let this be a beginning taste of what it would be like to defy your husband after we are married. For surely, as a purchaser of cattle would want to test their quality, you will want to know what a spanking might feel like from me."

"I understand what you're saying, but I've not been spanked in over ten years. I told you.

I do not find myself in trouble."

"Annalise, has your stepfather never laid a hand on you?"

"Well, yes. He has struck me across the face, but Charles has never spanked me or whipped me or," she added with contempt, "raised the cane to me."

"And I might do any of those things if the infraction was severe enough. However, I will never strike your face. I am not cruel, and that would be a personal attack. Discipline is not about the worth of the person, it is about the naughtiness of the choice. Now I'm going to sit in this chair, and you're going to come to me and place yourself over my lap to allow for the spanking. And if you do not, then I will accept that as your refusal of my proposal. I caution you to think carefully, my girl."

Stephen sat in the only chair without side arms. He watched Annalise for just a moment contemplate her decision, and then she slowly but steadily walked towards him and stood to the right of him. She reached her hand out in a silent request for assistance, and he held her steady as she gracefully, more gracefully than he had expected, leaned over his lap. He assisted her in settling before he tossed up her skirts.

Annalise's sudden intake of breath alerted him to her startle. He rubbed her back and reassured her. He didn't attempt to move her undergarment, for that indeed would be unseemly until they'd spoken their vows. He did see that she had only the light chemise under her gown and marveled at how she could stand the cold as long as she had. As expected, there was no garment under the chemise.

He lifted his hand and allowed it to fall, leaving a small stinging reminder of its placement. Annalise's movements stilled, and there was some stiffening of her muscles before the next smack made contact with the same spot. Her wiggle became a little more pronounced, but she settled quickly. He landed two more on the other cheek.

With similar crisp, quick slaps, he continued, feeling the flesh of her bottom through the inadequate covering. He was unable to gauge how pink her nether cheeks were becoming except by her inability to remain silent and the heat from her nates. Gesture and acceptance having been fulfilled, he tossed her rear end higher by lifting his knee, placing two sound smacks striking the under portion of her cheeks to her accompanying squeals. He carefully lifted her up to stand between his thighs and dropped her skirts, allowing her to put herself back in order. As he stood, he leaned into her, kissing her full on the lips.

"I'm proud of you, Annalise. You did very well." She smiled a watery smile, not having succumbed to a full cry but certainly coming close. "Stay here, my love."

Stephen went to retrieve the minister, thereby giving Annalise a moment to compose herself. He returned with the minister.

"Are you ready, my dear?"

The tone of his voice brought the tears back to her eyes unbidden, and she responded in a wobbly voice, "Yes, my lord."

The tears that followed her words began to overflow her eyes, trickling down her cheeks as they each gazed at the other. Stephen's heart melted. She was truly beautiful and absolutely everything that he wanted in a wife. Of course, she was not experienced in anything, but that worked in his favor and was to be expected. He would have to teach her, and that gave him a delight that he had not expected. He had become apathetic about running his estate. He had the thought that he would never be apathetic about his life again.

He was happy in his lot in life, but he'd become bored. This young lady would give him more than enough things to occupy him, and she would keep him on his toes. When she was ready, they would begin to fill their nursery, but not before she was settled in her own home with her comforts addressed.

Stephen reached up with the handkerchief from his pocket and gently wiped the tears from her face while he leaned down and kissed her lips, to the shock of the minister. Stephen didn't care. She was going to be his. He would kiss her if he so desired. His ardor at claiming her was building and his kiss hard. She whimpered.

"I'm sorry, sweetheart. I didn't mean to hurt you. I would never mean to hurt you." He leaned down and kissed her cheek. This time, as she looked up, she gave him such a brilliant smile his heart melted once again.

She crooked her finger to bring him down again to her level. "My lord, does that mean that you do not intend to thrash me again?"

"Oh, no, that most assuredly does not, my sprite. What it does mean is that I will take you over my knee, but no other may do so."

"But I don't want any more spankings."

"I am sure you do not, but it is a good method to teach a naughty young lady how she is expected to behave, such as now."

"But I am always good."

"I am sure you believe so, but you were not good today, sprite. You disobeyed me. I told you I would remember the insolence, and I did, but we have already discussed it. It is over."

She nodded and then looked up with her red-rimmed eyes and her tongue tracing her lower lip again. Stephen put his thumb over her lip and traced the line that her tongue had just left. He saw in her eyes that which she probably had no idea she was showing him, Her arousal.

Her eyes had darkened. He certainly knew his manhood was out of control and he needed to change his thinking immediately before he unmanned himself.

He turned her around to face the minister and said, "We are ready. Are we not,

Annalise?"

She spoke barely above a whisper, "We are, my lord."

The minister brought in several people he had in another room waiting in case the marriage did continue. They would witness and sign, attesting to the validity after the ceremony was over. He proceeded with the special license in hand to marry the two. The clergyman seemed anxious to accomplish the deed. The quickly performed vows were complete, and Lord and Lady Thayer left to begin a life Annalise had no idea about.

Stephen helped her get into the carriage and wrapped the blanket that was on the surrounding seat. However, before long, it was obvious she was still cold. Frighteningly so. She leaned into the carriage door, and he pulled her into him. After a second of resistance, she allowed him to draw her close so that she could gain some warmth from his body as well.

"I don't feel well, my lord."

She was still cold and shivered with very little control. Stephen was worried about his new little wife. She had been cold too many times today. When the carriage arrived at his home just off Mayfair, he accepted help to alight from the carriage. Walking up the stairs with her in his arms, he shouted as he ascended the staircase. She was half awake and half asleep, shivering the whole way up to his bed.

"I need hot tea, warm blankets and an iron cozy for the end of her bed. Bring them to my chambers." This was not how Stephen typically spoke to his servants, and it was understood that something was urgently wrong.

Earlier in the day, Stephen had come in and, with high energy and purpose of thought, went about gathering things from his office and gave very specific instructions to the housekeeper as well as the butler. He sent messages to his father and to his brother and quickly left again.

Stephen had known that the staff had been curious about his strange behavior today. He had no doubt that those he had in charge of his household had informed the rest to not gossip, but Annalise would still be a mystery until she met them formally. And the fact that this young lady was now being carried up the stairs by his lordship would start the chatter again. If there were strict guidelines concerning gossip before this happened to keep his lordship's house running smoothly, there was even more now. Even so, Stephen spared not a thought in that direction. Annalise was ill.

The housekeeper, Mrs. Thorpe, knocked on the door and came in as Stephen waved her over to him. "Mrs. Thorpe, this is my wife, Lady Annalise Thayer. I know this must be a shock to you, but there it is. There will be many changes in the household, but right now she has a chill and a fever. We need to bring her back to health. Please inform Mrs. Roundtree that we will most likely require more broth and tea later. I will take my meal in my chambers."

"Yes, milord. Should I turn down her bedding so her ladyship can be placed in her bed?"

"Oh, no. Annalise stays with me. Here. If you have any remedies for chills, please attempt them as I have waited too long for her to come into my life. I will not lose her now."

Mrs. Thorpe quickly took in all the information that her lordship gave her, left the warm blankets and was exiting just as one of the kitchen maids was settling the tea tray. His lordship asked her for his decanter of brandy, which he intended to add just a bit to her tea. The chambermaid left quickly to do his bidding. All evening the fever raged until finally, in the wee hours of the morning, it broke for good and Stephen fell into a relieved, exhausted sleep.

EARLY THE NEXT MORNING, the sun was bright; the air was still slightly warmed by a fire, but it had died down in the last few hours. Annalise was awakened by something heavy next to her. She was still a bit groggy and not quite aware of her surroundings as her thoughts on yesterday's events slowly began to creep back into her brain. She turned and saw Stephen lying in bed, and she screamed hoarsely.

"Lord Thayer, what are you doing in my bed?" Annalise looked around and amended. "Whose bed am I in? And where are my clothes?" And she looked down to an unfamiliar chemise and declared in a stage whisper, "I am undressed."

"Calm down, my dear, you are not undressed, totally, you have an undergarment on. You are in my bed as you were sick last evening, and you are my wife. Sleeping in my bed is not unheard of for married couples."

"Oh, yes. I had forgotten." She amended her statement, "I had forgotten that we were married, not that there were things between a man and his wife that were done in bed." Her eyes flew to his in horror. "We didn't. I mean, I would have known, surely."

He chuckled and stretched. "No. I assure you, you will know when we do. But as we are speaking of it—"

"Oh, please let us not speak of it, I beg of you." Her eyes were downcast and her hands worrying the bedspread.

He lifted her chin to effectively bring her eyes to his. "As we are speaking of coming together, I assume it is too much to expect that you understand what that actually means. Am I correct?"

"Yes. I mean, no, I mean, I don't know what that is precisely, but I have seen dogs, well, you know. Is it like that?"

"Only in the crudest sense, my dear. I will educate you as it should be. Now come next to me and let me make you warm again. The fire hasn't been stoked. It is quite early." He made to bring her into his arms and snuggle down with her when she pulled back again.

"But should someone come in—"

"Should someone come in, they would know that you are my wife and right where you should be, my dear. Now mind me, sprite, and snuggle in. You should get more sleep. You were very ill last night."

"Oh, but I'm not tired," she announced just before she yawned. "Really, I'm not."

"Well then, maybe it is time to teach you of those activities you missed last evening."

"I could sleep if I tried hard, I assure you."

He smiled and yawned. "Good."

She laid in bed but could not seem to find a comfortable spot. "I can't sleep. You should let me up, so I don't disturb you, my lord."

He sighed. "I know, sweetheart, just lay with me while I sleep, will you?"

"If you like, my lord."

"Stephen or Papa when we are alone, little one."

"Oh, but is that seemly, my lord?"

"Yes, my love. Alone, we have only ourselves to satisfy."

"I had no idea. I haven't had a papa in such a long time. It will be lovely to have one, but how can you be my papa and my husband?"

"Shush, now, let Papa sleep. I will show you and answer all of your questions, but first you must sleep."

"Yes, but... Oh!"

"Sweetheart, Papa, does not want to tell you again. You must obey me."

"Stephen, that hurt," she whispered again.

"Sleep. Now. Or it will be much worse for you, my chatty little sprite."

"Yes, my lord."

"Annalise."

"Yes, Papa, I mean Stephen. I know," she said as she laid her head in the crook of his arm, "shush."

She snuggled in tight, almost sharing his skin, before she sighed and kissed his chest shyly. He smiled, kissing the top of her head.

Annalise went back to sleep quickly, her slow, steady breaths pleasing him. He would have to show her how to separate their play time from the rest of their day and the world. He was sure that once they got past her thinking of what was proper, she would get as much out of the play as he would. He always enjoyed the teaching, but for her, he would be meticulous because it was for keeps. He needed to make his plan first. Sleep, now that not only his mind but his cock had come fully awake, came much harder for Stephen as he worked on his next steps. First was to settle her daily schedule for this week and then pack them off to the country.

Chapter 6

Annalise woke up again with the sun brightly streaming in through the open curtains. She did not need to reorient this time, but she did feel sadness that she awoke alone. The fire had been rejuvenated, and she felt a warm glow. She'd never had her own bedchamber since her father had passed away and she had to leave her family home. It became her uncle's inherited home and title. Her mother had told her only a limited amount before she married her stepfather, and she could only remember a few things about her father.

What she had was a small artist's rendition of her parents together in a locket her mother had kept for her. She found it in the pocket of her own coat after her mother died. She knew that it'd been her mother who had secreted it away for her. Annalise had kept it hidden and safe. She brought it with her yesterday. Maybe she could find out more about her father and now that she was a proper lady, introduce herself to her uncle. But that was for a later date.

For now, her thoughts concerned her new husband. What did Lord Thayer say about playtime and adult time? Did all married couples have those things? Excited about looking around and finding out what her new world would entail, she started to climb out of bed. It was high, and she was not overly tall, so she slid to the floor with a thump. And hungry. She was famished, for she had not eaten since the previous morning save a few sips of broth the evening before. She looked for her dress and could not find it.

She searched for a few more moments when she realized her first order of business of her need to relieve herself and wondered where she would do that? The room was incredible, with its rich décor. Annalise found a large armoire, hoping to find some clothing for herself but found only Lord Thayer's clothes and near it, she also found to her delight, a chair with a clean chamber pot for use. Happily completing her task, she cleaned with one of the cloths. Grabbing his lordship's grooming brush, she brushed her long blonde tresses and with nothing available to tie it up, she left it long.

Looking outside into the hallway, Annalise saw no one. Hunger was driving her forward. Therefore, in nothing but her thin chemise, she grabbed the throw off the sofa found in his lordship's sitting room, wrapped herself tightly, and entered the hallway. The throw was quite long and covered all it needed to, but she knew it was still not proper. She was as quiet as she had learned to be over the years so as not to disturb her stepfather. Her bare feet made her steps soundless. Therefore, no one heard her go down the staircase.

However, the stairway opened into the front foyer and who should be there but Lord Thayer with another gentleman who turned to see the little waif slipping silently towards them. The gentleman spied her first and cleared his throat, causing Lord Thayer to turn and look. Gone was the feeling of security she had enjoyed earlier and the fear that she had been seen by a gentleman caller to her husband took all adventuresome thought from her mind.

Looking up, it took a moment before he responded, and in that time, Annalise had come to her senses, screeched and turned to return up the stairs.

"Annalise."

She paused at hearing her name, but then she raced like a frightened rabbit running from the dogs. Tripping on the throw several times, she fell hard on the solid wooden step, hitting her knee. She attempted to scramble up before she felt strong hands grab her and hold her tight. A stern voice belonging to her new husband came through her panic and stilled her frantic movements.

"Annalise, stop."

"I'm sorry, I'm sorry, my lord. I just needed... I don't have my clothes, and I don't have my shoes. I can't find them. I was going to find a crust of bread. I—"

"Hush. Listen to me. Quiet. I should not have left you alone for so long. I'm sorry. Let me get you upstairs, and I have a new dress for you."

"You don't have to do that."

"Your husband expects to take care of you, and whether you are wearing clothes for Papa or clothes for Stephen, I will always provide for you. Now we will finish this conversation upstairs. You have two rooms, but for now, I believe I will keep you in mine."

"Why?"

"Because it pleases me to keep you near."

He pulled the throw from under her body and untangled it. He then lifted her up while having her hold the woven material. He draped it over her so she had some semblance of modesty and carried her up the remainder of the stairs to his chambers to the accompaniment of her pleas that she could walk. As he brought her to his room, she marveled at his strength and could feel the hardness of his flexed muscles.

Sitting her on the bed and admonishing her to stay put, he left her while he attended to the clothing issue. Annalise screeched again when the door opened to admit several maids with hot water, and a woman she had never met before. The woman was all business and tsked her for making such a racket.

"Who are you?"

"Come, come, my dear, you need a full bath, and I will help you reach all the places I am sure you will require assistance with," the stern woman replied.

Annalise decided she would put her foot down, although she was quite hungry and thirsty and a bit woozy in her need. She would speak as close to a refined lady as she could muster and bathe herself.

"Thank you for the offer, but I am quite capable of cleaning up on my own." She waited for the woman to leave and, remarkably, she did not. "Excuse me? Is there nothing elsewhere that needs your attention? I have said I do not require your assistance and will not say it again. Thank you." This time, she all but pushed the woman out of the room and the remaining maid followed.

Annalise enjoyed the hot water and wondered if it was her first full bath since she was a small child. She only remembered hand bathing since leaving the manor. While that was adequate, this was divine.

Annalise heard the door open again. "I said to leave me. I do not need your assistance. Go away."

"Is that the way you speak to me?" demanded Stephen, as she heard him lock the door resolutely.

"Oh. My lord, I didn't know it was you. I'm sorry. I thought you were that horrid woman." She paused. "I am undressed, sir. Completely, you surely need to leave or turn away."

"Good, I need to have a proper look at you. Why are you bathing without assistance?"

"I know how to bathe, my lord, and there is nothing proper about this."

"Papa or Stephen. I think we will begin our lessons now."

"Lessons, my lord?"

"We are alone, Annalise, and when we are alone, what have I instructed you to call me?"

"Papa or Stephen, but how am I to know?"

"And that is the first of our training."

"What training, sir?"

"There are many things that you need to learn, my dear, and we will start with when you are to call me what. First, I need to wash you up before the water has turned cold. My, this is quite dirty. You were grimy, my little sprite. You will need another tonight before we retire."

"I'm sorry, Stephen. I can't remember when I last sat in a tub full of water. I was a small child in my father's house, I believe."

"Yes, well, you will have one regularly now, my dear."

"Wonderful, but I reiterate, I can bathe myself."

He rolled up his sleeves. "Yes, I daresay you can, but you will not deny me the pleasure of looking upon your loveliness. Now, hand me your sponge."

She had already washed her hair immediately after she climbed into the water, while the water was still hot and clean. The soap was sweet smelling, leaving her hair and skin fragrant.

She grinned up at him, forgetting she was naked as he soaped and caressed her body. He started at her neck, soaping, massaging, and rinsing before kissing every spot he cleaned. He moved down to her breasts, repeating the procedure but suckling each one gently, smiling when hearing her swift intake of breath, followed by a moan of pleasure.

Her face was hot, and her eyes were sleepy as in a fever. Annalise had never felt anything so incredible before. "Stephen, what is this you are doing to me? What is happening to me?"

"It is passion, my dear. It is just the beginning of what you will have with me. We will share our passions and bodies soon. Just lie back and let me finish with your bath."

"Yes." When his hands touched her *there*, in the most private of areas, she squealed and looking up into her new husband's face. She knew it was not acceptable, the squeal and the touch. She tried her best to relax without much success until he began to rub her.

"Annalise, this is your pussy or cunny. Right now, I will show you one of the things that makes this a treasure trove of delightful bits. Just ease yourself and let me show you. But for all our sakes, stop your screeching, woman."

She nodded and tried to relax. The pressure built slowly at first and then it seemed as though she could not slow the tingling, the sensitivity of her bits. Stephen was looking at her intently as his one hand continued its onslaught on her nerve center while his free hand reached up to gently roll and tug on first one nipple and then the other.

"I feel like something is going to happen. Something must be wrong."

"Oh, no, my sweet, everything is right. Let it happen, my love, let it happen."

Just as there was an explosion of feeling in her body, Stephen tweaked her nipple, putting her into deep release. He kept rubbing but without her notice until she began to come down from the experience. Then he stopped. Leaning down, he kissed her lips so tenderly that she didn't realize when her mouth opened and he slid his tongue inside.

They tangled and mingled while he continued to kiss her. She couldn't help the moan that escaped, surrounded by several whimpers, before her muscles tensed a second time. She saw more colors behind her eyes squeezed tight.

Finally, he released her lips to her heavy sigh. Annalise gradually opened her eyes and saw his slow smile.

"Your water is cold, my dear. You need to get out now. We will do this again."

"Soon?" she asked wistfully.

"Oh yes, very soon. Now up you go."

Annalise noticed she was naked again as she stood before him. "My, um, Stephen, I do not have any clothes or covering, and it is simply not done, even if you are my husband."

He held up the large towel and invited her to step into it. He gazed into her eyes when she hesitated and said very calmly and with great clarity, "Learn this, my little sprite. When I say something, you will not argue with me. In our own house, in our own bedchamber, we do as we want. However, when I am taking care of you, no matter where that is, your only task is to do as I bid. Do you understand? I need you to trust me enough to allow me to care for you, protect you as is your right to expect from me." He held up the towel again giving it a shake when he saw her shiver in the cold.

"But..."

Her sentence never completed for her hesitation was met with the great slapping sound of Stephen's hand landing on her bare, cooling, and very wet arse. Screeching followed.

"Please, please, stop. Ow, ow, I need you to... ow." Her tears flowed.

"I will not repeat myself. I will not allow you to do that which may harm your health, nor will I allow you to be disrespectful. Now step out."

This time, she stepped out so quickly she sloshed water onto his trousers. She began to cry harder, for she knew he would spank her more for the carelessness. However, he did not seem to notice as he started to dry her with the soft towel.

"It is important to do as I say immediately, or you may find yourself with a stinging sit-upon."

"Yes, my lord."

"Stephen."

Annalise replied, "Yes, Stephen," as she cringed, awaiting his punishment for her lapse. It didn't come.

"Sweetheart, I am not an ogre. I do not chastise for things you do not know, and it would be tyrannical if I spanked you for every infraction. An occasional swat for attention, yes, taking swings at you for every infraction, never."

When he told her to lift her arms as he continued to dry her, she hesitated, still confused about the events of the morning. She felt herself at sixes and sevens. Her hesitation prompted his offer to continue painting her bare backside, and she quickly complied. When he was done, he brought her to the mirror, and they examined her body together.

"All right, sweetheart, I need to see you. No, sprite, don't hide. You are beautiful. Look at yourself. You are so perfect for me." He swiped at the tears still coursing down her cheeks, slowing but not yet stopped. Stephen ran his hand lightly down her collarbone, following it to the center. "I intend to place many beautiful, jeweled pendants to stop right here."

He touched the beginning of her cleavage and ran his finger down into the cleft of her breasts. The tremor Annalise experienced did not have anything to do with the chill she'd felt earlier. It was Stephen. Her husband brought that quiver to her insides. He turned her to face him.

"We will have our lesson as I see you." He continued to follow the contours of her breasts, neither too large nor too small. "These beauties are perfect for holding," and he demonstrated by balancing their weight in each hand. "Flawless." He continued to kiss her pert, stiff nipples, his hum of satisfaction demonstrating his love of how they drew even tighter together. She turned her head to the left to gaze into the mirror. "See how your nips are so excited to be loved?"

His eyes met hers in the mirror as he leaned into them and took first one succulent nipple in his mouth and then the other, leaving her yearning for more.

"Yes, Stephen," her response but a whisper caught on the hitched breath of her ratcheting emotions.

"You are Anna or Annalise to me when you are my very grown-up wife, and we are not in company or entertaining. Do you understand?"

"Yes."

"Excellent. Now, in all the places you are Anna or Annalise, I am Stephen, which is when we love each other, as we are doing now. When I make love to you, of which you have no understanding..."

"...except for dogs..."

"Yes, except dogs, my little sprite. I will make you forget those dogs soon, my love. We will also use our Christian names when we are with family and close friends." His breath was hot on her chest as his lips moved back up from her breasts. "Take my lead if you are uncertain."

He moved her damp hair aside as he kissed the column of her untouched neck. Annalise knew she was being consumed on the inside, incited by the other disturbances her husband was creating on the outside. He traced his fingers down her soft belly before diverting them towards her hips.

"In the places that I call you Lady Annalise or Lady Thayer, which will predominately be in front of the staff, when we are with guests, or entertaining, you are to reciprocate when you refer to me. Understood?"

"Yes, sir." Her sniffles were now fueled by the inferno her husband was stoking. Her whimpers at the unaddressed aching could be heard over Stephen's soothing voice. She hesitated and Stephen kissed her cheek, wanting to do so much more. However, it was imperative they get through this first bit of training, and so his cock would wait for a short time.

"And finally, when I call you Leesie, then you are to call me Papa." He placed his tongue in the outer shell of her ear, darting in and out several times as he met her eyes in the mirror again. He smiled when she cried out. "You must listen, my pretty. I will never call you Leesie in the presence of anyone except Mr. and Mrs. Thorpe, Mrs. Roundtree, your maid when we pick one and my valet. If we engage someone to assist you in some of the more womanly skills, then possibly they will know. It is for our entertainment only. If either one of us makes a mistake or finds we are not in the mood for that particular play activity, you merely refer to me in another way, and I shall do the same. If that should happen, there is no questioning the choice until we are in our bedchambers alone. Understood?"

"Yes." She didn't really comprehend the whole part, but she accepted the veracity of his statement and would tease out the intricacies of the meanings later. She did not want to incur discipline, but the thought of a spanking right now melted her insides.

"My lord?" she said, her voice quivering.

"Look in the mirror, Annalise, and watch my hand land on your bottom. You must use the proper addresses starting now." He turned her to the side, and she didn't want to, but she was drawn to the mirror and what it would reflect. She didn't even protest. Her heart raced.

Chapter 7

Stephen watched with fascination as his wife's eyes dilated with desire. She watched with rapt attention as they both followed the reflection of his arm raise and sweep down, slapping skin on skin. He rubbed the offended part with his hand and she closed her eyes, undulating with the circular movement as he fondled her nates.

He repositioned Anna and slowly raised his other arm. When the same treatment was administered to the other buttock, she released a sob, her eyes closed again. She made no move to step away. In fact, he was certain she had swayed back a few inches. He ran his finger down her bottom and up through the divide between the cheeks. While tempted, he did not want to bring her out of her euphoria with her inexperience. Stephen reached his hand beneath and between her thighs, where he had teased her to her first orgasm.

Touching her muff of coarse curly nether hair, he found Annalise to be very wet, soaking to dripping. He circled her bundle of nerves and then squeezed as he also gripped one cheek that sported his dark red handprint. Annalise stiffened, and he felt her belly spasm on his supporting arm that held the invading finger as she cried out. He worried her little nub until she needed his full support.

Scooping her up in his arms, he allowed the towel to drop from his arm and laid her on the bed as he ripped the clothing from his body anxiously. She still needed to be relaxed when he took her the first time. He wouldn't hurt her or tear more than was necessary, but he did need to penetrate hard enough to break the barrier. She was his to protect and his to love. He'd never taken a woman's innocence. This was momentous for both of them. He would be careful.

Naked, he swooped in and drew one nipple into his mouth, massaging the other as he slid her to the center of the four-poster bed. She arched towards him, almost causing him to come right there. His lovemaking became more urgent, and she responded with equal abandon. It was time. He could do slow the next time, but this was all he could hold out successfully for.

"Annalise," his low, rumbling voice spoke near her cheek. He took her lips, then released. "I am entering you now." She seemed to try to come out of the bliss she was enjoying in a more conscious state, and Stephen positioned himself at her entrance. She was so wet that he slid into the snug spot smoothly. He tweaked her highly sensitive clit and continued to press forward. "Here I am, sweetheart."

He circled her nubbin carefully and methodically, leaning down to support his upper body on his one muscular arm while taunting her breasts with his mouth. She tightened, lifted up and as he felt her begin to scream her orgasm, he flicked her nub hard and placed his mouth over hers as he shattered her virgin barrier. He stopped all movement immediately to allow the pain to subside. His mouth swallowed both her cries of ecstasy and shock.

He lifted up and saw her eyes were open but drowsy. Those were the eyes of a satisfied lover and he intended on seeing that look often.

"Are you all right, love?" She nodded as he wiped the few tears from her cheek. "I'm going to move now, sweetheart, the pain is over. That was the worst of it, and it only happens once."

She nodded again, but sucked her lip inside and held it between her teeth. Stephen eased her tortured flesh out as he began to move. Slowly he rocked, giving her time to relax enough to enjoy this ritual ride a little before he spilled his seed. He slowly slid all the way in and pulled all the way out to orient her to the rhythm and to stretch her sheath surrounding his cock. Her shocked cunny began to come back to life, so he increased his movements.

As he approached his release, he was awed by the responses of his inexperienced wife. She was so reactive to his ministrations and those of his body that she began to writhe and squirm as he picked up the pace. The pressure was painful. His cock head was purple as he withdrew and hard as a rod plunging inside her virginal space, making a nesting place for himself.

His bollocks were tightening and drawing up into the fire that started in his belly. The heat spread over his whole body, only to concentrate and shoot hot and straight as an arrow down his spine. Then the tingling moved up from his balls to meet in his cock. The tension was painful bliss. He tantalized her tits, teased her bundle of nerves couched in her anxious cunny, and slapped the flank of her buttocks and thigh as he stoked the embers of arousal. She heaved off the bed, causing him to quickly reach under to her bottom and hold tight, so she didn't unseat him and was delighted when she wrapped her legs around his middle as he rode to his release.

ONCE AGAIN, ANNALISE awoke to an empty bed, but the sheets were still warm, so she thought Stephen must have left only moments before. He returned, followed by a maid who carried a water decanter to exchange the one that was in their private sitting room that she had not been able to explore as of yet. Never mind, she thought. Stephen said we'll be leaving soon, but it would have been nice to know where I could have found water. I must be more assertive. I am sure it is required of the lady of the house.

Before she could get up to get some water, her husband sat on the bed. "I have asked for another bath for you. I don't want you to be too sore, for we will need to travel in a few days."

Annalise turned when the door opened, watching them bring in her hot water. Her voice became discreet. "Yes, I imagine I shall be tender, my lord. My muscles are crying out now."

"Yes, but I don't imagine it will last too long," he murmured back with a gentle smile. He watched the chambermaids leave again. "I will leave you to your bath, then."

"Mmm, before you leave, do you think I might have something to drink? I am parched. And perhaps something to nibble on if it isn't too much trouble?"

"Of course, my dear, you have but to ask. It has gone one o'clock, and we have done a monumental expending of our energy, have we not? Certainly high time we had a bit of tea. Well, finish your bath, and I will return for you. Be quick." A substantial kiss later, Stephen was gone to summon tea.

Her bath was so relaxing, but her tummy was more demanding than her aching muscles. She had soaked in a special concoction that Mrs. Thorpe had poured into her bath. Annalise got out when the water was too cool for further curative results, feeling much better. Bless the housekeeper, she had taken the sheets away too. Annalise had been shocked to see the smears on the sheet and her thighs but knew it was to be expected. She had spoken to some of the young merchant's wives. The worst would have been Stephen seeing it. Her mortification would have been complete. She shooed the women out of the room again as she dried herself, only to be joined by her husband again. Privacy seemed to be something no one expected.

"The fire has been stoked, so you should not feel cold, but if you do, you must tell me. I don't want you getting another chill. If you don't tell me things that you need when I find out, I will consider that a lie, a deception, and will punish you quite harshly, do you understand, Anna?"

"Yes, Stephen. When is tea coming up? I am quite famished."

"Soon, my poor, neglected sprite." His smile radiated to hers in the mirror, and she answered with a slightly crooked one of her own. She was a quick study, and that was important on these first lessons.

He kissed her neck as they looked in the mirror at each other. "Have you ever pleasured yourself before?"

"W-what? N-no. What a horrid thing to ask me. You may not ask a woman such vulgar things."

"Sweetling, this is our sanctuary. Remember that we can do anything, say anything in here. No societal rules apply. You know, I have never been with a woman who did not know how to pleasure herself. I promise to teach you everything you need to know. That is how it should be, anyway. I may be away on business and you have the need, but you must first get the rules of engagement or you will not be allowed to bring yourself pleasure without me." When she tried unsuccessfully to suppress a tremor, his tone was sharp.

"What did I say about being cold and not telling me?"

He moved to turn her to the side, giving his hand ample room to connect solidly with her arse when she turned and looked into his face and pleaded.

"Please, wait, I don't know if I am cold or if it is something else. Something you have taught me to feel. See, my arms are not cold."

He touched them, caressed them. Anna felt her cheeks flame. Her lip went into her mouth to suck on, and he reached up to pull it out instead of spanking her. He traced her cheek along the jawline before lowering his hand. He continued to speak as though they had not almost had a discipline session.

"Oh, sweetling, it is going to be such a pleasurable journey you and I will embark upon. Now, let me help you put on this dress." He indicated the rich rose-colored gown on the bed that she had not noticed before.

"Must I wear all of these petticoats? They are lovely, but I won't be able to walk well, and they will take up incredible amounts of space to get through a hallway. And this," she said, grabbing a scrap of clothing off the bed, "I will not wear." Annalise held up a pair of split bottom pantalettes. Her grimace was quite noticeable.

"Because you are not Leesie, I will allow the grimace, but should you find yourself in need of making that face while I am Papa, expect a thorough punishment. Do you understand, young lady?"

"Yes, I understand." She felt that yearning she could not name again at the word papa. "Please, Stephen, I do not wish to wear this. Please do not make me, milord."

"No, I am not a convert either, my dear, so how about we leave these for when you are Leesie? Then sometimes you will need to wear them because of the attire requirements. I shall not have you bending over without covering."

"I do not understand."

"You will. But we are not discussing any of that today."

"The gown is unsurpassed, sir, and I will wear it with a petticoat if it pleases you. But please say I may wear only one."

"One might be too cold, my dear. I see you disagree. Well, wear one for inside and two for outside in this cold weather. Now, the next thing I should tell you is that I will not tolerate any misbehaving no matter if you are Lady Thayer, Annalise, or my Leesie, do I make myself clear?"

"Yes. But I am an adult and do not misbehave."

He led her back to the mirror and turned her to the side. "Have you forgotten why your bottom has had red prints across it today?"

"So that you could bed me, my lord?" she wiggled her exposed cheeks.

He slapped her bottom playfully but spoke with a bit of sternness. "Cheeky brat, you behave."

Annalise laughed the first full laugh in jest since she awoke the day before and met Lord Stephen Thayer. She was gratified when he joined in.

"Now, we are returning to the country at the end of the week. Well, to be perfectly accurate, I am returning. You are newly arriving, so I need to have you measured and fitted for new clothes. That should happen shortly. I should suggest pantalettes until the measurements are over. Your sensibilities might be disturbed otherwise."

She blushed. "Yes, milord... Stephen," she quickly corrected.

"Good girl. Toiletries should be addressed as well. I assume you have none. I will order the basics. You will get any treat you like." He continued for a few more moments while she finished dressing, to include the knickers and then there was a rapping on the door.

"Ah, tea has arrived just in time for my famished bride. Come." With that one word of permission, a flamboyant woman and a small entourage entered the room.

Once the woman had a few words with Stephen, chaos began. Annalise tried to follow directions and forget her gnawing belly and dry throat, but it was difficult. She attempted to stop and eat several times, but the few crumbs that entered her hands were all but slapped away. She did get a swallow of tea before that was whisked away as well. After picking colors, styles, and placing his own order for his bride, Stephen had already slipped from the room to allow the measurements and other decisions on necessities.

Annalise was feeling a bit dizzy, and she felt sure it was from all the chaotic activities and the newness of the day. She felt sharp pangs of hunger, but the fact that things were not calm was what she attributed to the accompanying light-headedness.

"Please don't jostle me so. It is making me dizzy." They calmed down, and she thought nothing of it again until she found herself quickly turned back towards the mirror to see some jewelry. It was then that the room flipped oddly and her consciousness floated away.

Chapter 8

Stephen heard his name called, and he ran to assist. When he bounded up the stairs and entered the room, he couldn't see Annalise at first because a group of shrieking women surrounded her. He was sure she must be at the center of their noise, so he loudly dismissed all but the housekeeper, Mrs. Thorpe, who had entered ahead of him.

"What happened?" he demanded to the designer who had stayed in the room.

"She said she was dizzy and not to move her so quickly. We tried to comply but," the woman shrugged expressively, "when we would show her jewelry, she fell. Ah, see, she is awake again. Women, they faint, no?"

"Thank you, mademoiselle, but if you have your measurements complete, then leave her to recover. If you have more questions, write them down. Mrs. Thorpe, I believe Lady Annalise might still be ill from her thrice chill yesterday. Get me some water." He lifted Anna, who was awake enough to protest. "Shush. I am putting you to bed."

Which he did and covered her nearly naked body. He dismissed Mrs. Thorpe and assured her he would call for her if she were needed. He stripped his boots off and took off his outerwear to generate heat. She began to awaken fully after only a few moments. She slowly gained her equilibrium enough to giggle.

"We did this already," she observed as she snuggled into him. "And a girl must wonder if she will ever be able to wear a full complement of clothing with you around, sir." He smiled gently. "Darling, you fainted. Are you all right?

"I am now."

"Did you hurt yourself?" He looked at her partially clothed body, presumably for bruises.

"I don't believe so."

"What do you need to feel better?"

"Well..."

"Yes? Show me where?" He looked at her limbs again.

"I'm not hurt. I'm terribly hungry and thirsty, however, if it isn't too much bother. I never got my tea."

"What? It was delivered." Confusion was written on her husband's face.

"Yes, well, the seamstress and her aides were so intent on my measurements and fit that I never was allowed to have my tea."

"Unacceptable. I should not have allowed them in before you had it."

"Well, my lord, I don't think you were given much of a choice to decline madam's entrance." They both smiled.

Stephen took on a somber look again. "Tell me what you had for breakfast, darling; it must have been too little to cause this much trouble that late tea makes you faint. Unless you are sensitive to delayed meals and I will remedy that situation right away."

"No, I am quite accustomed to having tardy meals, usually because I have lost track of time, but I must have at least one." She looked at her husband sheepishly. "Umm... I didn't eat this morning."

He sat up straighter and said, "Oh, you must have forgotten, darling, think now."

"I did have a piece of bread yesterday morning with marmalade and a nasty cup of tea last night and the bit of broth you gave me, but that was it."

"That was brandy, sweetheart, not merely a cup of tea. You must have just forgotten what you have eaten. I'll ring for food right now."

When the full story was told, Stephen was angry. "I should have noticed. I left you to fend for yourself, and that was wrong of me. New rule, you must always eat your meals and bring it to my notice when that has not happened."

"I thought that I would be able to get a bit of bread or something, but it never happened. I'm sorry I messed everything up, but I thought tea was on its way. And when it came, so did the whirlwind, whisking away any attempt to partake of the tray that entered almost unnoticed."

Finally, a full meal arrived, along with some lovely hot chocolate for Annalise and tea for Stephen. There were also two glasses of ale that Stephen insisted they drink first to fortify her. It was more food than Annalise had ever seen at one time placed before her. She had already had one glass of ale and one of water by the time she turned her attention to the food and hot chocolate.

She turned and looked at her newly acquired keeper, said in wonderment and disbelief, "Is all of this for you and me, just the two of us?"

"Yes, I know that it looks like a lot of food now, but you haven't eaten for quite a long time, sprite. It is important that you eat well. I have no idea of the quality of food you had before this, but I'm quite certain it was not of the same class. That will change as of now, of course. I intend to take care of everything."

"Is it not my responsibility to take care of the domestic tasks of the house? I will not purposely refuse food when I am hungry, my dear. Of that, you can be assured."

"I don't intend to leave it all to chance in the beginning. And your duties do not even present until you have settled into Thayer Hall."

Annalise watched him as he cut up her food, a meat and vegetable pie, and began to hand-feed her like a little bird, using a spoon at times and his fingers at others. Before this moment, she would have raged at such insolence. She would've felt degradation at being treated like a child. Now there was a warmth attached to it. There was caring and nurturing that indicated love, not infancy. She had almost forgotten how it felt to be well cared for, to be cared about, and she couldn't help but allow the indulgence.

"And your parents, do they live in Thayer Hall as well?"

"No, they live on the other end of the estate, a goodly distance, in Thayer Manor. I am quite happy with Thayer Hall and may never move into the manor once father has passed. Mother will live in the place if we do not. I love my mother, Annalise, but a man should not have to listen to her incessantly. If she is ill, that will change the situation, of course."

"Have you any living relatives? I should have stopped to ask earlier, to be sure, but I assumed not."

"I do have, or maybe had, an uncle, the second son of my grandfather, my father's brother. When my father died, Uncle Charles, now Lord Coton, came to relieve us of the burden of our manor and to assume the title father left behind. I imagine he will live there still." Annalise continued with tea as though it were of no consequence.

"That is why you have some distinct mannerisms that are inbred. It is also why you are equally comfortable without their use."

"Possibly. I lived there until I was nine. I am not sure about the next year, but mother then remarried. You know how that turned out."

Stephen nodded thoughtfully and then changed the subject.

"It is important that we finish the conversation about what happened this morning, though," stated Stephen. "This is a conversation that is imperative. We will learn each other, I promise, but until that time, you must tell me if there is any need that remains unfulfilled.

This could have been a very serious issue if you had gone much longer without nourishment. You're not to do that again."

Annalise looked at him as he stared back at her, clearly waiting for her acknowledgment and response.

"I can take care of myself, Stephen."

Her stubbornness was coming out once again. It was a comfortable place for her to be indignant, and she used her irritation to cover frustration and to hide her insecurities with her situation.

"It is my job to make sure you do, so learning to ask for what you need and not let the world roll over you. That will be an excellent start."

She ignored his words. "I am not sure how I am going to fulfill my promise if I don't know the routine of the house, my lord. It will be difficult for me to ask for more of something, for it is not how I was taught to behave. If I don't have what I need, doing the best I can with what is readily available to me without asking for assistance is the only acceptable way. Now you are asking me to be needy and require others to do for me. It feels wrong, my lord."

"Excellent point, my dear. We will stay here a few more days while we are packing things up and, unfortunately, there is nothing to do but to be here and begin to learn each other. You will find that once we are back on the estate, that leaving others to do their job will not feel as though you are burdening them but allowing them to do what they do best. That is when the real education will begin."

"Education?" Annalise's eyes squinted as she worried about what that truly meant.

"Lessons if you will." Stephen popped a few more pieces of food into her mouth before he continued. "There are so many things that you need to know that you do not. You don't know how to be my Anna, nor do you know how to be Lady Thayer. However, I'm quite confident you have every idea of how to be my little sprite, all rolled up into my Annalise. Moreover, neither you nor I have a full understanding of how all of this is going to work. But I assure you all mystery will be solved after we go back to the estate in the country, for we shall solve it together."

He leaned over and kissed her cheek, taking the napkin and wiping the crumbs from her mouth. He gave her a gentle smile as she responded with a shy one of her own.

Stephen sat straight again, and his tone strengthened. "I need to explain to you the consequences of not telling me everything if your needs are not being met. You will be placed over my knee, and I will smack your bottom quite soundly. I will always spank you until I feel you understand the error of your ways. Your needs must be communicated, or I cannot keep you safe."

"But you cannot do that routinely. I'm not a child."

"You forget, my dear, I am your husband now, and while beating your wife is not acceptable to me or anyone of any conscience, correction and discipline are quite acceptable. Things are going to be very different for you now and for me. I know this is all confusing to you, but I promise to help you grasp it all. Just give me time."

"I want to finish feeding myself, thank you. I'm quite well and quite capable." Annalise sat up straight and reached over to grab the fork on the tray, suddenly appearing uncomfortable. She watched Stephen as he slapped her hand.

"If you don't want the next slap to be on your bottom, you will not pick up that utensil."

Annalise quickly looked up into Stephen's eyes and was quite positive he was telling the truth. She held her hand up above the utensil and allowed him to hope for a moment that she would do as she was instructed. However, the sprite in her needed to still test him to find if he were a man of his word. She made her decision one of defiance instead of compliance.

Her hand began to lower to the fork while she stared him straight in the face and watched his expression. She was disappointed because he did not waver in his combined look of seriousness with the full expectation of obedience. It was the mere fact that she knew he had no doubt that she would follow through on his edict, that she did not.

Quickly Annalise dropped her hand onto the fork and snatched it off the tray. Almost instantaneously, Stephen stood and removed the meal tray from the bed, walking quite sharply to set it on the side table with a distinct clatter. She could hear the china clang against itself as it rocked and then settled back onto the tray, thankfully all still in their previously upright positions. ***

Stephen walked over and very precisely slid the fork out of Annalise's hand, and she gave no resistance. Her eyes were open wide, and it was apparent her uncertainty was rampant. She didn't know whether she could trust him. He knew that. She also was not ever blithely going to accept life as presented, simply because another said it was so. He liked that. She was not afraid to test him. He loved that.

Annalise was still in a state of predominant undress since the interruption to the fitting occurred. It was unfortunate for her, for it made her quite easy prey to his now itching hand. It would entail no battle to uncover her. She would learn defiance would be met with discipline.

Without another word, he sat on the bed, reached his arm around her waist, and drew her over from a sitting position to an aligned position, prostrate over his thighs. To this point, she had made no resistant move, as though she were frozen in place once she had touched the utensil. As soon as he had her in position, he had drawn her shift up and began to untie the awkward pantalettes intent on baring her earlier tenderized backside. She screeched. Her exposed skin met with cooling air, pulling her out of her daze and Stephen saw her expand on his lap in full fighting form.

It was only then that he believed she understood what had happened, and that payment was about to be extracted for the act.

Wholly unfazed by her rambunctious activity of rolling and kicking trying to escape, Stephen landed a solid echoing slap, immediately blossoming his handprint to red. He could almost hear her processing the spanking, but not in an altogether logical format, it seemed, for she continued to fight what she had earned.

He knew that had Annalise any rational thought, she would have concluded this was not the best position in which to be defiant. But that was not the case. His little sprite was tough, and he liked that about her. She had good body strength, and he knew it would allow her to birth his children well. However useful and reassuring this related information was, it was not why she was over his lap. She must learn to yield to him, and he did not believe it would be an easy lesson.

"I believe that was a Leesie response to my admonishment to allow me to feed you. That will not be tolerated, my little sprite. Defiance will always be met with discipline."

Another hard, loud slap painted another handprint on her other cheek, and it was at this moment that her writhing and fighting stopped. Stephen watched her accept the pain. Now that she had stilled, he knew the intensity of his spank seared through her fleshy globes, forcing her to acknowledge it and its creator. It was at that point that a sniffle escaped her lips.

She entreated her new husband in a small, anxious but very contrite voice, "Please, Papa, please do not spank me. It hurts. You are hurting me. I'm sorry I disobeyed."

Stephen paused in his total surprise at the change in his lovely sprite. Gone was the defiant imp she had been moments ago. He could have almost smelled her fear at the retribution when she'd made the insubordinate move. Now she was calm, albeit sniffling, contrite, and polite in her begging for pardon and relief. She had called him Papa naturally. He was overjoyed.

He almost stopped with just two swipes, but he didn't want to have to address this again. If he stopped now, he would most definitely have to readdress the defiance later. He knew there was more behind the act. It was a calculated move, deliberate. She needed to test his merit, test his trustworthiness. It was his job to be worthy of her, to be of great substance. Because he had warned, he must follow through. Therefore, as hard as it was for him, he responded to her as she needed, though he did so with gritted teeth. He raised his hand again.

"I know, sprite. Papa understands, but I need to make this lesson good so that we don't have this question again. When I instruct you to do something or not to do something, that is your law. You must always do as you are told. If you defy me openly, Papa will always have to punish. You understand?"

"Yes." Her next question had him choking back his own apology. "I understand that I am not the wife you wanted. I don't know how to be all the things you are asking, but if you are not too disappointed in me, I would like to stay and try."

"Oh, my love, you are just the sort I want. I chose you. There is no one that I need more than you. This is new for both of us and will take some time to find our happy rhythm. I have never had a wife nor you a husband. And I do have my particular desires that will take time to make right for us, but have no doubt that I will never let you go. I am quite convinced you are perfect for me and I will do my best to be perfect for you."

She answered in the same meek voice she had used in her apology and her begging for him to not hurt her. "Please do not spank me too much. It hurts dreadfully."

"I know, sprite, lessons can be painful, but I will never cause you an injury. You are mine. What is mine I take care of always. But I also chastise, and that is what this is, nothing more and nothing less."

The spanking began in earnest. He knew she had not experienced many spankings, so he didn't dilly-dally about administering it. He firmly tattooed one cheek and then the other with the same precision as the military marches. Soon his love was crying in earnest, and it hurt his heart.

He needed to finish quickly because all he wanted to do was cuddle her and let her know how much he loved her. He did love her, not fully, for that would come with time, but he loved this woman-child. He would have never guessed how much. She had no idea how hard this was for him, and he had no notion that it would be this hard for him. Reminding himself that this was going to cause her much more grief if she didn't get this lesson quickly, he completed his task.

Smack after stinging smack rang out as he meticulously covered every inch of her wiggling, trembling globes, tipping her forward to make sure that she received his whole message by also covering the tops of her thighs. As hand spankings went, it was a profound one. She was a blubbering mass of salty tears, slobber, and sweaty, matted hair by the time he was through with her instruction.

She had cried and drooled all down her face into her blonde hair, darkening it. She was heaving as though she had run a great race and was crying as though she were heartbroken to have lost that race. Stephen gathered her up into his arms. Taking his hot and throbbing hand, he moved her plastered hair from across her lovely face and tucked it around the back of her ears.

He took the napkin that had been left on the bedcover and wiped her tears before leaning down to kiss her eyelids. He crooned to her and rocked her to reassure himself as well as his woman that she was well. He sighed with relief as he felt her snuggle into her place on his chest; she was meant to be there. It was as though she had always been there, in his arms, drawing comfort from him through her hiccups and sighs.

He brought his hand down to her bottom cheeks and could feel the heat radiating off of them. She whimpered. His chest tightened, his heart seized. For a moment, he felt remorse for having been the cause of her hot buttocks and tears. He had to remind himself that he wasn't the cause, her actions were the cause, and he was the deliverer of the consequences of those actions.

She would learn. They would be good together. He tenderly rubbed her insulted flesh, drawing out a moan he was sure was arousal.

"Papa wants you to take a nap now."

"But I didn't finish my food or my chocolate." Things were back to normal. She was trying to assert her authority by whining her manipulation. Suddenly she stopped and looked at him as only his Annalise would. He smiled. Good girl, learn but don't abdicate your place.

"I promise to get you a fresh tray and nice hot chocolate after your nap."

Annalise sat up and looked at him with a look of consternation on her face. "But that's so wasteful. My lord, while it was pleasing hot, I promise I can have it cold without ill effect."

He looked at her quite intently to meet and match the seriousness of her statement. "I'm quite sure you can. Nonetheless, I don't choose that you do. I choose that your food is warm."

And as he saw that his Leesie was going to respond in a contrary manner he lifted his eyebrow giving her a look of disbelief that right after her spanking she was going to be disagreeable again. Annalise must've gotten that message, for she slapped her hand over her mouth before she nodded and lay down on the bed. She turned and grinned up at him. His heart seized in desire. How did he ever live without this woman in his life?

"Come in with me, my husband." Gone was the sprite Leesie. In her place was his wanton wife, Annalise. His cock jerked to life.

"No, I have too many duties to accomplish today. My bride, however, has had other ideas for the majority of this day. Do you think she would take a nap so that I might finish my tasks, safe in the knowledge that she is resting in preparation for dinner and later, her husband's attentions?"

"Well, with such a lovely manner, I am sure he could convince her to allow him that peace of mind."

"You are incorrigible, and I can't seem to get enough of it. Go on, wench, rest."

He patted her still warm bottom and smiled when she squealed. He pulled the covering over her, and she snuggled into his pillow, deeply inhaling his scent before readjusting one last time. Sighing, she closed her eyes. Stephen watched her for a little while after she had gone to sleep, finding himself falling deeper and deeper under her spell. The spell she seemed to have no idea she was casting on his heart. His life would never be the same.

Chapter 9

"It's time to get up, my lady. His lordship would like you to get dressed in preparation to meet dinner guests." Annalise watched the young girl open the wardrobe as she yawned and stretched leisurely. The maid was not much younger than Annalise was, and she decided she liked her.

"Oh, hello, what is your name?"

"Molly, ma'am."

"Molly. I like that name. You say it is time that I should get dressed. Yes, all right, however, into what I'm sure I can't imagine. Will any of clothing I brought with me suffice?"

"I shouldn't think so, milady."

Annalise tried to remove the sleep from her eyes and the dryness from her throat. She could see that the maid had taken the tray and felt a bit sad for she wanted that chocolate still. But her memory as to what Stephen had said returned and was glad the temptation was gone. It was going to take quite a bit of effort on her part to temper her choices and not give in to the things that she would have given in to without his influence. Like cold chocolate.

It was then that she acknowledged to herself that she would never even have had the opportunity to enjoy the chocolate hot or cold if she had not been with Stephen. It was not so difficult to acquiesce at that remembrance.

"Then what shall I wear? Oh, right, I could put on the gown that I had earlier. It's very elegant."

"Oh, that would never do, my lady."

"Wouldn't it? That seems rather ridiculous to put on a fresh one. Of course, it will do. It's the finest dress I have ever owned. Do you not think it's beautiful enough? For if it isn't, I have nothing else to wear." Annalise felt that would be the end of the conversation, for she truly had no other gown.

"You do have other gowns. And a lady never wears one that has been mussed before it is freshened."

Annalise sat taller in the bed as she swung her legs out from under the covering and had to practically slide off the bed. She would be more careful this time. Was there no stool to help her climb into or out of this monstrosity? She wondered briefly, why a bed was so high off the floor but then left that thought to address the chambermaid.

"That is poppycock. There is absolutely no reason why I should not be able to wear that lovely gown." In truth, she had fallen in love with the dress and would have consented to wear it every day. It was the most beautiful thing she had ever worn.

"Lady Thayer, Lord Thayer informed me that if you were to put that gown back on instead of putting on a fresh one, he would not be happy." The girl delivered the information quite innocently, unknowing the implication of retribution those words carried.

Annalise huffed out a frustrated breath while she quite dramatically flung her arms to indicate the room and said, "Then where is this magical fresh gown I should be wearing?" She knew she shouldn't be rude, but she felt very ungracious at the moment.

The young woman silently walked over to the wardrobe and opened it just as Annalise had done earlier in the morning. Anna sported a smug smile, knowing full well that, except for the little satchel that she brought with her, and the dress of her mother's she'd worn here, the cupboard would be bare. However, when the doors were opened, the wardrobe was full. It had seven gowns all hung very meticulously on the clothes rod. Each gown was a different color and all complementary to her creamy coloring.

Annalise's hand flew to her mouth to try to hold back the escape of the joyful cry at seeing those gowns.

"They are all so lovely, but they aren't mine." Just at that moment, there was a rap on her door, and the door handle opened, admitting a surprised Lord Thayer.

"Annalise, my love, you need to get dressed. My father, brother, and sister-in-law shall be here soon. It seems they delayed their leaving until tomorrow, so you may meet them tonight. What dress have you picked out to put on, my dear?" Lord Thayer began to look around the room to see if he could locate the one laid out for her but seeing none, he looked back at Annalise's face. His expression was one of question, not irritation.

Annalise stared at her husband with her own look of confusion. "My lord, these are not my dresses." She put her hand out again to indicate the wardrobe and all the possessions within. "Where did they come from? And how did they get here?" She ended her questions with her hands on her hips as though she would demand an answer; however, her countenance was still in awe.

"My dear, they are making the rest of your dresses and will send them to the estate once they are done, but for now these are all that they had either partially done or were already done but the adjustments to meet your specifications." He walked toward the wardrobe.

"In this case, it was quite fortunate that they had several that they could quickly alter to fit you, don't you think? At any rate, you need to get dressed. Your maid here can help you, and you should let her. This is not a formal occasion, so any of those dresses would be perfectly appropriate."

His tone took on the warning that she was learning to identify quickly as he leaned in to speak intimately in his wife's ear, effectively making the conversation completely private.

"You have thirty minutes, and I shall be back to escort you no matter what your state, sweetheart. However, I can promise you that if you are not dressed, we shall have another conversation when our guests have left. I'm sure you're not interested in that happening."

He stepped back to speak openly once again so that the maid who had taken a discreet few steps away could hear him. "All of them are beautiful, my dear, but I particularly like the blue one. I believe it will match your eyes."

Annalise looked at the maid again and said, "Then I shall wear the blue one." She turned and looked at her husband as he smiled and walked out the door.

Stephen was as good as his word and appeared promptly at her door to escort his nervous wife down to meet his family. While Anna felt a little worried about meeting Stephen's relatives, she soon felt at ease. His father, Lord Radcliff, had quite a dry sense of humor and seemed intent on keeping her smiling while his brother, James, was not as intense as her husband. He was extremely solicitous towards his wife who was anticipating soon by the look of it, and she appeared to be quite happy with his ministrations. It seemed as though he were doing it up a bit too brown with his attentiveness. But what did she know about the ways of the aristocracy?

The one thing no one mentioned was where Lady Radcliff, Stephen's mother, was. It was as though she didn't exist except when they rose in response to the dinner announcement. Now who would escort Mother in?" asked James.

"Well, it depends, brother. If she were nice to Annalise, I would and allow Father to escort my wife, but if she were rude, then I would bring in my beautiful wife and allow Father to take Mother in."

"Yes, well, Father better inform Mother of the rules of etiquette in your house now you have a wife so that she makes a decision she is willing to live with and so are you."

"Oh, I would never upset the order of things," Annalise assured the others.

"Yes, well, that is considerate of you, my dear, but if Mother cannot mind her manners, she is delegated to the second seating." Annalise looked horrified. "I wouldn't actually do it but it would be a good lesson. She is seldom allowed to go for too long before Father reins her in."

"Oh." She didn't know what to make of that, but now she worried about her reception with the matron of Stephen's family.

As they approached the dinner table, Annalise's discomfort rose again, for she'd never seen such a grandly set table except in paintings. The fear struck her that this was a simple family meal. The color drained from her face slightly as she thought about having guests, real guests. How much more elegant would the setting be? She knew none of this. This was all a mistake.

What was she doing? What was she playing at, thinking that she could be the lady who Stephen expected to run such a grand home? Moreover, this was just the London house. She had been led to believe that this residence was nowhere near as grand as Stephen's estate. Maybe she should back out now before she embarrassed herself or Stephen anymore.

Her husband, ever vigilant to her changing moods, quickly slid his arm around her waist and guided her to her seat on the right of him. He pulled her chair out and directed her to her place, sliding her close to his position at the head of the table for comfort. He seemed to make a concerted effort to have his hand touching her often, to give her security that he already knew she was lacking.

He didn't know everything that she was thinking by far, but she was positive that he could tell that she was ill at ease. Some of the lessons that Annalise knew her husband intended that she participated in would most likely take that fear away. Experience, familiarity, and practice itself would do the rest. She hoped.

Before he took his seat, he leaned down to her ear as his family was finding their seats and whispered, "Follow my lead. Pick up the utensil that I pick up and use it the way I use it. You're doing quite well." He kissed her cheek before taking his own seat. It was a public display of affection that was often frowned upon in normal societal circles. His father nodded in approval, and Lady Thayer gave him a nervous half smile.

As the evening wore on, it became easier to relax, and by the end of the evening, Annalise felt tired, but quite accomplished. As they returned to the bedchamber that she now thought of as their room despite the societal norms of separation, she fairly danced through the door, throwing herself on the almost too high bed in exhilaration.

The maid, Molly, had said it wasn't seemly for her to sleep openly every night with her husband. She said congress was something that was understood but not acknowledge in polite society. But her Lord Thayer did not seem to be of the same mind, but she should try to stay within societal norms. His words broke into her thoughts.

"You were wonderful tonight, Lady Thayer. My family was quite impressed. I fear I shall have no peace once you understand all the intricacies of being Lady Thayer, for I feel we shall be constantly entertaining."

He was teasing her, but she also saw his pride in her ability to play hostess. Pride wasn't something she remembered others feeling in association with her. Oh, she was quite sure her mother had been proud of her, but things had become quite complicated once her father had died. Then, once they were tossed out of their home and her mother had married her stepfather, it was Charles' opinion that he was the most important person in her mother's life. She mentally shrugged all of this off as she often did through the years and looked at the dashing man standing before her.

"Why thank you, kind sir. I believe you might be right. But it was solely due to your kind intervention." Annalise got off the bed and started for her rooms that Molly had shown her, just through the sitting room, through the connecting doorway, unbuttoning her dress as she went when she felt his hand stay hers.

"THEN IN REPAYMENT, my dear, would you allow me to undress you this evening? Tonight, as most evenings, I want you here with me, Anna. Do you object?"

"No, but isn't it against societal norms?"

"It is, but do you care?"

"I feel I should, but I don't. Shall I send my maid away then, sir?"

"I'll ring and tell my valet."

That chore dispersed. Stephen reached up and kissed her neck as he unbuttoned the top button. He slowly kissed her back, relishing as each button was released from its binding, tasting the smooth, fragrant skin beneath. Gently, he moved her hair to the side, running his hands through its silky smoothness. It was pure heaven and one of the greatest luxuries he had experienced in his lifetime. He didn't even attempt to stifle his moan as he buried his face in its golden strands.

The buttons were undone, and she had no knowledge their release was complete until he pulled the straps of her gown off her shoulders. She allowed it to slide as he held the material and continued its downward motion until free of her body and it fell limp to the floor. Anna felt that she too would be sliding limply to the floor to accompany it, supportless and unable to give structure. She was a mere shell of her outer self as her inner self melted into his caresses.

He removed her dress from the floor after helping her to step out of it. Anna swayed slightly as though keeping her balance was a challenge, and indeed it was beginning to be one for him as well. She swayed back towards his fingers that drew the undergarments one by one from her body. He reached for her breasts, tweaking nipples that were so hard they were small torpedoes of lust. He massaged their firmness and the blushing skin surrounding the nips, offering them up with pride for his mouth to suckle.

"Present your breasts for me to suckle, my sweet."

"Milord?" a resounding slap answered her. "Ow, ow. What did I do?"

He lifted a stern eyebrow. "Who am I?"

"Stephen. This is confusing. You must give me time to learn."

"Privately, I am Stephen or Papa."

"Yes, I know, but I forget. It is early days, sir...Stephen."

He nodded. "You are closer to remembering now. Present your breasts. Place your hands under them and offer them to me for my lips to caress."

She turned into the heat of his lips as they suckled and kissed her breasts before walking the trail down her soft belly, placing trembling moist caresses upon her sensitizing skin. She shivered. He licked. She moaned as he returned to suck her nipple in again. He watched her skin flush hot and reached to find her thighs slippery with her honey.

"I want you to watch me disrobe, Anna. Then, I am going to love you with my mouth, my hands, and my cock." Stephen continued to explained to her what he was going to do and how he was going to do it, which both thrilled and frightened her. His words brought her to such a quivering mass that had he not picked her up and placed her on the bed, he was confident she would've been as a jellyfish, slithering to the floor without backbone to support her.

As she watched him, Stephen meticulously took off every item of his clothing and laid them on the chair, turning to present himself to her, expecting a response. Anna did not disappoint for her sudden deep intake of breath filled the room with the sound of awe.

"Say it, Anna. Ask your questions. Tell me what you want?"

"My lord, I didn't take all of that monstrosity earlier, surely. I mean, there is so much of it, him." He watched as she stared and could almost see her brain thinking and hear her thoughts out loud, although she said not another word. She scooted back just a bit, leaning against the headboard.

"You almost did. But the more we exercise that muscle, the more it will be able to accommodate my companion here. I'm going to join you in the bed, and you are going to touch me," he said as he got into the bed and stayed her hands from covering herself up.

"Give me your hand," he instructed, and as she reached her hand out in curiosity, he carefully placed it on his manhood. He cautioned her to be gentle.

"It looks angry." To which he laughed and allowed her to further explore.

"It is my cock. I can assure you that is excitement, not anger."

"It, um, your cock, is very warm, hot even. Does it hurt to be so hard? And turn purple?"

He moaned, for at the moment, it was almost excruciating. Taking Anna's hand from further exploration brought on a giggle and a whimper as though a dessert had been taken away before consumed to satisfaction.

"Lie back, Annalise. Let me show you how achy it feels." He inched his hand down to her thatch of hair. "I promise you will be happy that you allowed me to show you more of the wonders of being married. Spread your legs for me, darling."

"Milo-Stephen, that is unseemly."

"It is anywhere else but here. Behind our closed doors, and with your husband, it is all seemly. Do not forget."

"No, Stephen, I won't."

Chapter 10

Annalise awoke to sunshine and warmth. She was so content that she felt like hugging herself. She entered a new existence when Lord Stephen Thayer had brought her into his world. It was a domain that he shared with her. It was a world where she not only survived her first encounters of the marriage bed but also thrived in them. While technically it was the second night because the first night she was ill, there was nothing substandard about the realities of what she had experienced yesterday, twice. She was beginning to understand what Stephen meant when he said there was a Lady Thayer, Anna, and Leesie all rolled up inside Annalise. Because she was quite certain she'd been all three yesterday.

As Leesie to her papa, there were absolutely no responsibilities but to follow his instructions and to be a good girl. Both of which would be a trial on all but the most sedate of days for the firebrand, who she now began to identify as Leesie. The little one could be defiant. This carefree role she was allowed to choose at appropriate times, was indeed her papa's sprite.

Similarly, just as the mythical sprite was as prone to naughtiness as well as niceness, the Leesie in her was finding pleasure in both. She had lost that opportunity at a young age and it was, at times, difficult to be carefreely little, but the freedom it afforded her was unsurpassed. However, it was quite clear that the only cuddles Leesie would receive were benign, as an unmarried girl needs, not as a married woman expects. There was comfort in that as well.

On the other hand, Lady Thayer was, of course, exactly that. Stephen, along with his father and brother, had great holdings and responsibilities to the Thayer Field Estate and its inhabitants, all of which he took quite seriously. Lady Thayer would be expected to be the grand patroness of all of her husband's holdings, to include overseeing things such as baskets for the needy, celebrations at the manor, and to be an ornament on her husband's arm.

Her mother-in-law would normally be the one to orient her to the best way to accomplish her duties and would even be joining forces, but the marchioness refused to acknowledge her. Her mother-in-law was quite appalled at her son's choice of wife, according to her new sister-in- law, and declined to come with them to greet her or visit her at any time.

While the marquess was quite genuine in his approval of her as a person, she didn't miss the looks he gave his son. There was little doubt that the older gentleman was not sure he could understand why a man of Stephen's background and status would marry her, but he told his son she was enchanting within her hearing. Outside of what he thought she could hear, he questioned his son as to the throwing away of the advantage of marrying within his peerage. She didn't hear what her new husband replied, but he said his piece and came to stand next to her right afterwards.

She would do her best to win her new father-in-law over to her abilities as Lady Thayer as well. The rest, well, the rest was for her husband to deal with, anyway. She wondered if her father's title at the time of her birth would assist them in believing she was not too far beneath his son. And why that mattered so much when his son had been looking for a while before choosing her? Surely they would be happy that he had someone he wanted to spend his life with? Have a family with regardless of her lineage.

Annalise liked Stephen's brother and his wife best. James was open and honest. Elizabeth was quiet and unassuming, but her words were the undressed truth. While Stephen said he liked that type of clarity, he did not want his wife to practice it too strictly. He told her as they had a few moments after the guests went home to their beds to discuss the evening before retiring themselves.

"Some things are not meant to be said, truth or not. If it is edifying, then feel free to share your thoughts. If it is not, then refrain from saying it to others. However, to me, you may give me the untainted truth, with due respect, of course." He smiled.

Last night, James had been welcoming. "Lady Annalise, it is a pleasure to meet you. We received this frantic message from Stephen that he had found the woman he was looking for and intended to marry her before she slipped away. Could we stay a few more evenings so he could introduce us. I can see why now. Not only are you enchanting, but my brother cannot keep his eyes off you. It is a wonder he allows you to walk, for in doing so, you must touch the earth." He turned to his wife. "Don't you think our new sister is delightful?"

"Yes, but you are embarrassing her, James. Annalise, you must not allow my husband to speak so freely in your presence. He has no tact, the poor darling. However, no matter how smitten my dear husband and Stephen are, you must not expect too much from Lady Radcliff. She does not understand why Stephen would not marry any of the women she had chosen for him to consider."

"Elizabeth, do not be cruel."

"I'm not, James, I am realistic. Your mother is not here because she still hopes that Stephen will come to his senses before Annalise is anticipating, so he can petition for an annulment. If they find her in a delicate way, then there is no way to undo the vows. Lord Radcliff, do you think your wife would be more inclined if she knew that Annalise's deceased father was a first son? She tells me all she knows is that he was Lord Coton and because the family estate was entailed, it went to the second son. They were unceremoniously sent away."

"Dreadful. There are some who behave in such a way. Thankfully, it isn't common. It is possible the news could help, my dear, but I think we should allow things to happen naturally. Stephen does not reside in the manor as we all do. Therefore, it is less likely that she will be able to find ways to dislike our Annalise." He turned to Stephen, who had come up behind his new wife. "Mother only wants the best for her eldest. You'll just have to win her over slowly."

"And Annalise is the best for me." He looked at his wife, who had begun to withdraw both in physical stature and figuratively. He sat next to her on the sofa, drawing her close to his side as he continued. "And if Mother wants a relationship with us, then she will need to accept that I knew what I was doing and am unbelievably happy." He kissed his wife's cheek again.

What Annalise knew, encased with the expectation of being the lady of the manor, was the expectation that she would know all things that she was required to do, such as adequate benevolence to their tenants. From the other side of that role, Annalise had often been the recipient of benevolent caretaking.

She had often hoped that she would be able to repay those who had been so generous to her, and now she found that while she probably would never repay those who had given to her, she could be equally generous to others. She was still worried about her mother-in-law's reception, but it seemed she was the only one, so she put that aside for now.

However, the running of the household was another story entirely. Annalise had no idea which silverware to use when, how to do fancy stitchery, mending yes, embroidery, no. She had a singing voice of note, but performing was not something she had done since childhood. The pianoforte was minimally attempted, also in her early years. The years that she would have learned languages and how to run the large household were lost to her.

She learned sums and how to keep accounts in the shop, and while she could read, she did not enjoy it. It would take all of these things to meet Lord Thayer's requirements as his wife, and it was going to be a challenge at best. She would have to discuss with him how she would receive instruction without bringing embarrassment to him and preferably not much to herself.

She had approached Elizabeth, who eagerly agreed to be her private tutor on things particular to Thayer Field Estate, but nothing else. "I am still learning things I thought I knew. I can give you information particular to the Estate."

Annalise had suggested it to Stephen before even meeting Elizabeth. She asked her husband if he would object. He had advised she wait and see if she could get along well enough. Now that Annalise knew she did and had all but committed to the exchange, it would be another thing that she needed to present him with and hoped that he understood her need to have a woman help her. Besides, he was so busy and would be even more so once they were home in the country.

Leesie was a persona she simply was confused about, but it made her feel the most cared for. Her husband was adamant she was a naughty, enchanting sprite underneath her Lady Thayer and that excited her and filled her with trepidation. That young lady seemed to need more cuddles, playtime, and spanks.

Finally, the third persona she was to take on and indeed she had taken on already, was Anna. She felt this one would need the very least amount of instruction to be quite good at handling. Her husband had said several times to her that this job was to make him happy and to allow him to make her happy. But wasn't that the expectation in all areas of their life?

"Simply put, my dear, I require that you be a wanton in my bed."

She had first been shocked that her husband would ask her to be shameless. However, when she had experienced his brand of promiscuity, her objections were put to rest. Maybe being a wanton with your husband was acceptable. She certainly enjoyed it.

No day was as intense as the first full day she was Lady Annalise Thayer in the flesh. It was day 3 but her second wake up in her new life. Her husband evidently had more things in the business realm that he must now take care of since their marriage. He needed documents changed, both personally and in business. It had extended his stay in London. While it didn't seem to have disturbed him, he was intent on completing the business quickly.

"I am a prudent man, normally. I spend what I need to without remorse, but gambling and excessive drinking are not for me. I don't have a paramour any longer, and I certainly have little to do with things outside of my shire, for the most part. I will strive to make sure you have everything you need."

"You have already provided me more than I have ever had. I need nothing more, my lord, but you."

He drew her to his chest and kissed the top of her head. "That is why it is I who will take care of things this time. You would do without too much. I require my wife to be comfortable, not deprived."

"But I am certainly not deprived. And you should not take your time to gather more for me. I don't need it."

"Possibly, but I need for you to have them, so I will do as I please." He had kissed her, then landed an unexpected swat to her behind before leaving the bedroom with a whistle. He was certainly in good spirits today.

Therefore, she saw little of him in the days that followed. This saddened her, but it did make sense. He always brought her treats and new things to add to her travel trunks, which had grown from her satchel to three trunks already. She used the time to learn about his family lineage from a sampler on the library wall, reading a few interesting pages in the news, learning about the staff who was coming with them to the country. There was so much to learn.

She did receive a call from a young woman by the name of Lady Chantelle Moulton. It wasn't a name that she'd ever come across not that she had many opportunities to come across women's names anyway, but it was a shock when she came to visit since they had no previous acquaintance. Lady Moulton made it quite clear that she was engaged to Lord Thayer.

"Oh?" responded Annalise.

"How interesting that he has not mentioned you, and I assure you we are quite well acquainted."

Annalise correctly assumed that the woman's announcement was intended to call off any amorous thoughts that Annalise had towards Lord Thayer. She wondered what Lady Chantel Moulton would think if Annalise disclosed that unfortunately, the man she declared was her fiancé had, without consulting with her, apparently married another. She did not disabuse her of the understanding of why Annalise was in the home, however, choosing to wait for Stephen's explanation.

"I'm not quite sure who you are or why you are in my fiancé's home," stated Lady Moulton. "however, I'm quite sure you must be a distant relative of his. Stephen told me he had several distant female relatives who had yet to attach their affections to another. I can see he was quite right when he said they were nothing to look at or to spend any energy considering."

It was quite evident the rude comment was directed at Annalise, but as she had spent her own life avoiding such confrontations with equally rude and obnoxious people, she had no difficulty sidestepping this poisonous arrow aimed quite pointedly at her heart. Happily, it was quite a simple task for Annalise not to take the dangling bait; she was, after all, Stephen's wife.

"And when is Lord Thayer returning?" asked Lady Moulton when it was evident she was not going to get a rise out of Annalise.

"I can't be certain. We leave the city for the country at the end of the week, and, therefore, I'm positive he'll be back by then. However, the task of closing up the house will take most of his time, I'm afraid. I shall be happy to tell him you have called. And if you are, as you say, his fiancée, then he must speak to you daily, surely." Annalise was not above being a bit snippy and snarky when the occasion called for it.

"Oh, yes, but as you say, he has been busy arranging for his departure to the estate. It will be excellent, for I shall be leaving the city in less than a fortnight. We'll be able to stop on our way through to cement the arrangements. Shall I see you there?"

"Oh, I feel quite satisfied we will run into each other if you should come to Stephen's home in the country. Whenever you choose to come."

The effect on Lady Moulton upon hearing either her extended stay or the use of Lord Thayer's given name in such familiarity gave Annalise an unladylike feeling of satisfaction. A bit of smugness, even if she was not to refer to him outside of the family or very close friends as anything other than Lord Thayer. The woman did say she was his fiancée and, as Lady Thayer, or Annalise, or even Anna, his wife, wasn't that relationship close enough?

"Who did you say you were exactly, my dear?" inquired Lady Moulton.

Annalise very adeptly changed the subject to not be required to address it at all.

"As you say, a close relative. Oh dear, would you look at the time? I should be having a fitting in a few moments, and I do apologize, but I will have to take my leave of you, Lady Moulton. Stephen will be ever so cross if I miss it. I shan't be able to get another before we leave."

Good manners being what they were, Lady Moulton could do nothing else but take her leave. After she was gone, Annalise was concerned that Lady Moulton was known by the staff, and she did seem quite familiar with Lord Thayer. Annalise, having recently learned what familiar could entail, experienced a tingle of distress as to the implications of that familiarity. Did paramours visit their lover's homes? She felt certain they did not.

For while her brain told her it was simply a cat and mouse game that Lady Moulton had been playing with her, her heart was angry that there was such a situation in which the mouse and the cat came into any proximity at all. However, she trusted Stephen to have not led one woman on, only to become entangled with another.

Chapter 11

Stephen returned home seeking out his new treasure. He was taken aback when she looked at him a bit irritably.

"What in the world is the matter with you? I've taken my leave from you all day, come back eager to spend time with you, and you greet me this way."

His tone had turned to a more chastising one rather than the welcoming one that he had entered with. He held his arm out to welcome Annalise into his embrace, and she readily accepted the invitation. He leaned down and placed a hungry kiss on her lips before lifting up his head to give her a penetrating stare.

"Come have a seat with me, my dear." The wording of which was not a true request. "Sit next to me here on the sofa and talk to me about how your day has gone."

Annalise huffed a sigh but sat, anyway. Her fingers played with the front of her dress, not making eye contact with Stephen. Her husband was not having any of it and lifted her chin so that he could see into her eyes. She knew her face reflected her ambiguous feelings about the request to share, and she also knew why she was uncertain. She shrugged her shoulders not so delicately.

"I've missed you today," she began. "I had not thought it to be true so soon, but everything I look at and everything I touch screams your name. I missed the owner of that name. Otherwise, I had an educational day, learning all sorts of things from Mrs. Thorpe. Oh, yes, and I was diverted by my first caller. Well, she was calling on you, but I didn't think it would hurt if I tried to entertain her while you were away. Your fiancée decided not to wait for you but to meet up with you on her way back to the country."

Annalise's body had stiffened. She no longer looked Stephen in the eye but continued to clutch at her gown. She knew she sounded more affected than she wanted to but presenting it to her husband bothered her more than expected. Stephen released her face and reached over to stay her hands, helping her to release her skirt and spreading it out smooth again.

"That is quite a ridiculous tale you are prattling on about. I married you. I'm quite certain you were there when it happened. While you might not know everything there is to know about many things, I'm quite sure you understand that once a man marries a woman, there is no such thing as a fiancée. So now, who was it that came to visit you that you have now decided is my betrothed?"

"Well," Annalise resumed scrunching up her dress, and Stephen once again stayed her hands. Resolutely she straightened her shoulders and looked at him straight in the eyes.

"Lady Chantelle Moulton came to visit her fiancé and was quite surprised that I was here. She was quite free with her conversation about wedding plans and going to be married to you. I did try to nail her down on a date, and she did not have one, for she was waiting for you to help her decide. And then she gave me various time frames of the year that it might be most advantageous to seal that connection."

Annalise had become a bit agitated, and so had he.

"My Lady Thayer, you cannot expect me to believe that Lady Chantelle Moulton arrived at our home today, and blithely announced that she was engaged to me." The look of incredulity was unmistakable.

"Are you saying that I'm not telling the truth?" Annalise yanked her hands out from underneath his where it sat on top of her folded ones in her lap, jumped up, and pulled away from him in anger.

"Annalise, you are not allowed to respond to me in such a manner." Stephen knew his irritation was becoming quite evident as he also stood up from the sofa. Dammit, where did she get such thoughts?

Annalise looked at him, full of unbridled anger. She was so irate that Stephen could see that it clouded her judgment or she might have heeded his warnings, for he made sure it was evident in his words and tone that he was giving her a caution to calm herself down. However, instead, he watched her walk the circuit of the room in angry strides while gesticulating heavily.

"I am not allowed to respond to you in that way? Yet it is perfectly all right for you to call my words and character into question? There are few things, my lord, that you might have taken notice of in regards to me. One of them is that I never lie." She turned to stare at him and then resumed her furious pace. "I might show hesitancy in responding due to my expectation of the discourse, but I do not lie. I try to do things that encourage the non-necessity of prevarication but were it necessary to say something that I was reticent to say, I would still do so honestly. You do not have the right to call my words or me into query." She turned to face her husband. "Therefore, I do not wish to speak to you." This said in continued agitation as she neared where Lord Thayer stood and where she had begun her tirade. Her small foot stomped the ground to accentuate her words.

Stephen was no idiot, nor was he immune to the hurt and anger he heard in his wife's voice. He might have only been married seventy-two hours, but he knew that Annalise spoke the truth. This brought him to another question. Why would Lady Moulton declare such a misrepresentation of the truth?

"Annalise," he began and when he could see that she was not going to respond softened his tone, "Anna."

It had the desired effect. She slowed her step to a stop and looked at him, her frayed feelings still on display and her breathing still shallow but slowing. He put his hand out in invitation and watched as she hesitated. He left his hand extended in hopes that she would understand the full meaning of its offering. He felt a sense of relief when she put her own hand out to place in his. He grasped it firmly and drew her to him.

He leaned down and moved the curtain of her hair that she had left loose to gather behind her ear as he leaned down and tenderly kissed her. He angled himself back a smidge and traced his finger along her cheek and down under her chin, lifting her chin up to allow him to gaze intently into her eyes.

He knew he was already lost. He would love this young woman who was his dream made real for eternity. She had accepted things quite easily, much to his delight. He'd expected it to be quite more dramatic, and while he was not an ignorant man, he had hoped that there would not be much in the way of resistance. He could freely admit to himself that he was rapidly growing to love this woman. He would do anything to keep her content. That included keeping out the rest of the world, if it were necessary, to make her happy.

Never one drawn to drama, not on the stage or in his front parlor, he led his wife back to the sofa to tease out what must've been going on while he was gone. Further, to form a plan as to what to do should this occur again. Many mothers would be quite aggravated that he had looked over and found their daughters wanting. They would be amazed that the beautifulness of this innocent woman in front of him had ensnared his heart without design. It amazed him as well, but she captivated his heart so completely and so immediately that he gave not a thought to any of the other women offered him. How could he?

But that was obviously not how the other young women felt. It was apparent that on some level that at least one of them thought that the attentions he had given her entailed more promise than they actually had. As they sat on the sofa, he drew Annalise into the protection of his arms, helping her to lay her head on his chest as he played with her hair.

"I apologize, my dear. I do not question your veracity, and I shall be careful not to do so again. But I do need to understand the situation. I did not offer for nor make any feelings known that I desired Lady Moulton's hand in marriage. I have not offered or made my feelings known that I desired any woman save for you. It does disturb me that she made that announcement to you, a woman she had never yet met before. Is that correct?"

"Yes. She assumed I was a relative."

"Did you disabuse her of that notion?"

"Why should I? I would have stopped her from disclosing if I had."

"And did that good lady say why or under what circumstances this event was purported to have happened?" His words were still quiet and yet curious, and he hoped his tone was not lost on Annalise. He truly was confused.

"She did not say as to the exact event. And honestly, I felt that she declared that association to discourage me from setting my cap towards you."

"Yes, that makes sense. What you need to understand is there were quite a few mothers and their daughters who made no secret of their desire to form an alliance with me. However, I can tell you that I did not declare for any of them. In fact, the day that we wed, I had decided none of them would do, no woman in my acquaintance would do to marry. I had decided to leave town and to begin my search in the country." He leaned down and kissed the top of Annalise's head. "That was until I ran into you, my dear. My sassy, disobedient, independent little one."

"Is it because..." Annalise looked up hesitantly, as though deciding whether she would complete the thought out loud.

"Go ahead and say it, is it because—what?"

"Is it because you didn't think that anyone else would accept you as Papa?" Annalise had looked down at her hands, which had become fidgeting once again.

"Partly, I suppose. However, I think if I had found the right woman, I would have known that she was the one. You are special, for you alone, in all of my acquaintance are the one who has the talent, the ability, and the honesty to be able to be all three parts that I desire in a wife. You are more than I ever had hoped."

"My lord, what if you had not found someone?"

"I don't know. Most likely continued on as I have been. But I don't have to do that anymore, do I, my lady, for I have found you." He sat her up briskly and said, "Now that we have answered all of those questions, what are you to do the next time someone you don't know comes to pay a visit to you?"

"The staff seemed to understand who she was, and I didn't know she wasn't a relative or someone who had an appointment with you."

"Good points. In the future, if you don't know who it is, you don't have a scheduled meeting with them, and I am not here to receive them or decline them, you will instruct the staff to accept the card but not the person."

"That seems rather rude, don't you think?"

"Absolutely not. There are many people who would like to claim an acquaintance with me or, upon learning of my wife, one with her. There are unscrupulous men and even women in this world that would love to get you at a disadvantage. This will avoid that event. If someone comes unannounced, they should be prepared to be turned away. And if I find that that is not what has happened, I know a young woman who will find herself in a less than enjoyable position over her husband's knee. Am I understood?"

Annalise huffed and said in a less than fully compliant voice, "All right."

"Do you doubt the seriousness of my words?" He raised his eyebrows in warning.

"No. But if I am Lady Thayer at the time or Annalise, shouldn't I be able to make that decision?"

"Possibly, but for now I don't choose that you do. You sound a bit tired; did you get a nap today?" He effectively changed the subject, just as he had hoped he could.

"My lord, I don't take naps daily. That would be preposterous. However, I am quite bored, and am happy that you have decided to come home even if it is to bandy about edicts for your wife."

Stephen could hear Annalise regressing, and he wondered if she understood it to be her unconscious way of asking for nurturing and to be treated younger, lessen her responsibilities. He was becoming more and more of the opinion that they would not have to devise playtime. She would just fall into it when she needed it. That would be the best-case scenario for them.

They would leave the day after tomorrow, and he had luckily been able to finish all of his business, save for a couple of pieces which could not be addressed until tomorrow. He knew this was confusing for her with all the different roles. It would be clearer once they were back at Thayer Hall and she could take control of the household. She would be more than busy, and their dynamics would change.

The appropriate times to assume her roles were predominantly left to his decision for now. He thought he would give her a choice of being Anna or Leesie. He was through with Lady Thayer for the day with no other engagements and past the time for uninvited visitors. He felt with certainty that she was through with being the lady of the house as well.

"I wonder; do I wish to be Stephen or do I wish to be Papa for the remainder of the afternoon? What do you think, my dear?"

"Oh. I don't believe that you can be Stephen. It is still daylight. I certainly couldn't be Anna in the daylight. I don't want to be Leesie." her voice had changed even more so, indicating to him that Leesie was indeed who she wanted to be this afternoon.

"Oh, my dear, you have misunderstood something about these roles. Anna can be Anna at any time of the day or night at her husband's discretion or Anna's request. Later, I hope that you would be able to initiate being Anna whenever the need and the situation allow. I understand at this moment that would be too much to ask." He cuddled her to him. "I think I'm in the mood to be Papa, anyway. So let's go upstairs into our bedchamber and unlock that door off Lady Thayer's bedroom, shall we? I need to see what should be taken with us when we go, and I would like you to help me decide."

Stephen made the motion to stand up as he reached over to grab Leesie's hand. Leesie pulled her hand away so that he couldn't get a secure grip, rolling her body to the right of his to escape his reach. Stephen sighed and knew that she must need some extra assurance after the visit today, and structure and discipline often would give that to a sprite. He was aware that this persona would allow her to declare her confusion without appearing to be immature.

"Leesie, we are going now, and Papa will not allow you to show your petulance. Be a good sprite and Papa will reward you, but if I have to deal with a naughty sprite, I shall have to spank you."

He waited. He could see there was indecision in Annalise's body language, and thought he would help her out just a little by trying to distract her.

"You haven't been into the playroom, and there are ever so many beautiful things in there. It's a shame that you don't want to see it because then you won't get a choice as to what we bring back with us. And you could leave some charming dolls if you don't decide."

He extended his arm once again, encouraging her to take his hand. She looked up at him, obviously battling whether she should take his hand to be the obedient sprite or not take his hand to be the naughty sprite.

"Leesie, this is my last request. The good girl gets a treat, the naughty girl gets a spanking and a nap. You need to make a choice before Papa makes it to the door, because once I place my hand on the door, the decision has been made."

He was beginning to cherish this part of Annalise. He loved that this was a wonderful outlet for her to release all of her insecurities. It offered her the opportunity to learn to trust without reservation. For Stephen, it allowed him to give to her what he always had longed to do for someone who belonged to him, security in a paternal way but not as to his child, but his wife. He knew he would be different with his children. He couldn't say how exactly, but he was confident of that fact.

For he didn't have to play master of the house when he was Leesie's papa and he didn't have to use all of his manners and meet all the protocol when he was her papa. While she could let go of all of her insecurities, he could just love her without reservation and relax.

Stephen had already made it across the room, and in another step, would have to reach out and grab onto the knob. That, unfortunately, would mean that he would have to respond to his naughty young lady. The last stride was made, and he hesitated for just a second. As he moved his arm slightly, Leesie screeched. He sighed his relief.

"Papa, no, wait for me." She ran across the room to grab onto his coattails. "I don't wish to be a naughty sprite today. I don't want a spanking. And I would like very much to see in the playroom, if that would be all right." Since she had made the decision not to be naughty, her eyes were sparkling, and she fairly bounced when she spoke of the playroom.

Stephen smiled knowing that the transitions from one role to another would be rough and sometimes difficult for a while, but he could see that once they had eliminated those hesitant doubts about changing roles, things would settle down and be much smoother. They needed to get out of the city and go home.

Sometimes, Leesie would be able to stay in her day dress because she would simply be looking for cuddles and release of stress, but today was a full role switch. Once he had helped her change into one of the shorter dresses that required pantalettes, they would go into the playroom, properly attired, to choose the toys that Leesie would bring home. Tomorrow, they would pack up her clothing and all of her accessories along with his. The day after, bright and early, they would go to the country and that's when the real fun and the real work would begin.

Once the door had been unlocked and the treasures inside revealed, they played for quite a while, even having their tea in there once Papa had explained to Leesie over his lap that when he said no, he meant no.

"Over my lap, young lady, or you shall be very sorry indeed. I will put you to bed for a long nap on a very sore bottom. I said you have a large dollhouse in the country and, therefore, we are leaving this one here for when we come back to the city. You should be very ashamed that now you're going to have your naughty bottom spanked in front of all of your dolls."

Leesie's eyes got large and her mouth opened as though that thought had never occurred to her and now that it had, she was horrified.

"Papa, punishing me in front of my new friends would be so embarrassing. Please don't embarrass me," she whispered.

"I think it's too late to be worrying about your pride, my mischievous little sprite. What you should be concerned about is how hot your bottom is going to be and that you will still be required to sit on it. And that Papa is trying very hard to allow you to bring all the toys that he possibly can, and you are disrespectful and ungrateful."

His voice was stern, but inside he just wanted to squeeze her tight. Every moment he spent with his new wife gave him new joy. She fell into this play as though she had been waiting her entire life to do it or had been doing it her whole life. She had needed this, too.

"I understand, Papa," she said, using his often-recited wording, "I suppose you're right. Then can I turn my dollies away so that they don't see you spank my naughty bottom? I don't think they should see my bottom. It would be improper, and I don't believe that they should see me cry. They would see my bottom and see me cry, right?"

"I fear so. So turning them around might be a good idea."

By the time Papa had watched Leesie turn every doll carefully around to face the wall and assure them that she would be back shortly, he didn't have the heart to spank her anymore. But he knew he must do as he promised. So, without any further fanfare, she stoically walked back to him and climbed over his lap.

She shivered when he reached to pull down her pantalettes, and he decided only to separate the seat. She was so cute and adorable as he rubbed her bottom, getting it prepared for his smacks. The lecture came on doing what her papa said, when he said it, and by the time he had completed his speech, he was able to pop her lower cheeks just a few times and convince her to accept his words with very little effort.

He could see how hard she tried to be tough, but by the time he had finished, she was sniffling. He rubbed her nates again, kissing each one before closing her pantalettes up. He stood her on her feet to allow her short little dress to fall just below her reddened bottom and assured her she was his good little sprite and her naughtiness was all forgiven. Papa allowed her to have a small pillow on her chair so that she might enjoy her tea better. He was delighted with her.

With the task of separating and dividing the toys into two categories decided they settled the traveling toys in a wooden box to be transported ahead of them. That complete, it was time to leave the sanctuary of sprites and papas. Lord and Lady Thayer had final preparations to plan.

Annalise's dresses had arrived, and she laid them each separately across her bed in her own chambers. She had yet to do more than investigate her designated rooms, for Stephen insisted on her occupying his chambers with him, and she wasn't sorry about that. The placement of her new attire was so she would have the opportunity to exclaim excitedly over each as he approved of them. Now the gowns that Lady Thayer had at her disposal numbered ten, which Lord Thayer declared was adequate, but certainly not at all in excess.

Annalise, on the other hand, was quite exuberant. "I have never seen so many elegant and perfectly lovely gowns in my whole life. I was positive that some women must have this many, but I never thought I would. I am quite sure that I shall never need another gown in my life. Thank you so very much. You are too good to me." Stephen smiled knowingly and simply sat back to enjoy his wife's excitement. It gave him great joy to make her that happy, and he prayed he'd be able to do that for many years to come.

"Annalise, let us ring for them to be put back in your armoire. Or better yet, begin the packing of all but your traveling gown."

"Oh, don't do that, Stephen. I can put them back. I made the mess, after all."

"No, if you do all of your maid's work, she won't have a reason to work for me and will lose her job. So, for her sake, let her do things for you."

"Oh, Stephen, I never thought of that. Surely, there is so much to do that lightening her workload is a good thing."

"Anna, sweetheart, I know you want to help, and there will be times that you can, but your husband is in need of his wife. You wouldn't deny me some gratification, would you, love?"

Annalise laughed. "I certainly wouldn't want my husband to lack something so essential as his own type of play. Very well, call the maid."

Stephen laughed. "I wonder what has you so compliant, sweetling? Is it the still warm bottom that you are carrying or the remembrance of last evening that has created the urgency in your movements?"

"Both, and it is too bad of you to remind me."

Once the maid appeared, and the task had been assigned, Stephen took his wife through to his chambers and his bed, indulging in his pleasure after giving Anna some of her own. For the next several hours, they lounged and played until it was time to prepare for dinner.

As they went down to dinner, Annalise preened in one of her new dresses as Stephen gallantly escorted her down the stairs. "Dinner, as well as all our meals, would be at the same time in the country as it is in London when we are not entertaining or being entertained. Life is on a predominately regular schedule, and it is very similar to here."

He spent the rest of the evening answering questions, discussing all manner of things, including the differences between town and country living. Annalise was a little dubious about the necessity of so much pomp and formality, but seemed to accept Stephen's explanation that it is how it was done.

When Annalise began to yawn and show signs of fatigue, Stephen decided it was time for bed. "I don't know why I'm so tired these days. It is quite strange."

"You've not slept through the night since the first night we were married, my dear. I am sure that is the reason. And unfortunately, that may not change in the foreseeable future, so I would recommend a daily nap."

"Or my husband could sleep through the night and then I would sleep."

"True, but I highly doubt your husband is inclined to sleep all night for a good while. Better to learn to take naps than wait for your husband to change his new routine. I have it on good authority that he enjoys it so much, he may never change that particular schedule." Stephen kissed his wife hard. "Now, off to bed with you. I will come up presently."

Chapter 12

Lord and Lady Thayer arrived at their country estate in the late afternoon the day after they left London to be welcomed by a full staff. The trip could have been done in one long day, but Stephen didn't want Annalise to be too tired when they arrived. He had spent the extra time explaining what would happen when they reached the hall. What he didn't mention was that he intended to carry his bride across the threshold in keeping with tradition. Annalise giggled and then put her hand over her mouth because she knew that she needed to be Lady Thayer at this point.

Stephen leaned down and whispered in her ear before he set her down, "There will be no giggling, Lady Thayer. Only my Anna and my Leesie may giggle. So giggling will be allowed to resume after the introductions. Once we have discharged our duties, I shall be intent on assisting you in producing those giggles once again. So please be prepared."

He gave her a look of mock sternness before setting her on her feet. Annalise took a couple of seconds to bring her manner back into more formal mode as her husband, true to his word, introduced each staff member. He waited while she said a few words and he was quite proud of the way that she was able to present herself.

"I shall be showing Lady Thayer our chambers and familiarizing her with some of the routines for the rest of the day. We will have dinner at the normal hour, and if you would have a light tea for us in one hour, we should be most grateful."

Lord Thayer escorted Lady Thayer up to their bedchambers and proceeded to acquaint his ladyship with the comfort and versatility of his bed. Anna giggled often.

For the first couple of days, Stephen was intent on Annalise learning about her new home. To that end, he took her throughout the house several times, pointing out certain things that would alert her to the placement of the rooms. Such as his study was next to the library and should she be summoned to him with very few exceptions, she would be summoned to his study. The library was where she would be expected to read the books that he instructed her to read. She was not to question his choices, for they were to help with her education. Of course, any other book, in addition to his choices, would be perfectly acceptable.

"Must I read?" Annalise wrinkled her nose. Upon looking at her husband's scowl, she straightened her face quickly, giving him a sheepish smile to soften her question.

"So by your question, it mandates I ask two others. Have you learned how to read?"

"Quite a while ago, my father insisted. My mother loved to read. Although after Father died, we did not have many books. The ones we retained, Mother read them until they returned to dust. Personally, I don't want to read about how lovely the world is, how wonderful people are, or how I should be thankful for the smallest crumb of bread. While at times the world is quite lovely, and there are some people worth knowing, and I am thankful for all good things, I don't need to read about them."

"But surely, my dear, there are places that you want to know about and lovely adventures for women that would tantalize your thoughts."

"I'm sure there are. I simply don't want to partake of someone else's experiences. I prefer to have my own."

"Well, unfortunately, there are some things that you shall have to read, and I will query you on them, so it will be expected that you thoroughly attend to that which you are reading."

"Very well, however, you must understand that I go into this with great objection, and I don't like all subjects. I think it is unusual for a husband to want his wife to read."

Stephen tipped his head. "I will take that under advisement, my dear."

Once Annalise had proven that she could readily find the library, the study, the front parlor, all bedchambers in use, her husband felt more at ease to leave her to wander the house. Those rooms, in addition to the gallery, the dining room, kitchen, and lastly the playroom, were explored. Then Stephen felt she was informed adequately to begin her lessons on how to be his wife.

The training weekends began in earnest. Stephen's intention was to begin with intense weekend training and then she would practice the skills all week. The premise was a good one. The actual results of the first weekend were not as successful as he had hoped.

It began in the morning when Annalise was to start her day as Leesie. Stephen tried to prepare her the night before by explaining that the mornings would be to learn how to be Leesie with him when he desired or when she desired it and the afternoons would be for Lady Thayer.

"All right, and then when do I get to be Annalise or Anna?" Annalise asked with her hands on her hips in an irritated fashion.

"No matter who you are, that manner you are presenting to me will never be acceptable." He stood quietly as Annalise changed her stance. "Thank you. Now with Leesie in the morning and Lady Thayer in the afternoon, then in the late evening my wife will be my wife with no airs and no responsibilities other than to me and our pleasure."

"Yes, Stephen."

Bright and early Saturday morning Annalise was awoken from her night of delights with her husband to an energetic woman bustling through opening window curtains and making a grand row. Groggily Annalise responded irritably.

"Please, must you be so loud? I am not ready to wake up." Annalise pulled the covering over her head and reached over to her husband's side of the bed, finding it quite cold and empty.

"It is time for you to get up, my dear. It is training morning for you. It's time to get your day moving." The woman continued to bustle around and finally stopped in front of the bed, hands on her hips. She seemed to be demanding obedience by her stance.

"Yes, well, come back later. Much later," Annalise responded with a muffled voice under the covering.

"Oh no, my dear. Your papa said you were to remember this was his Leesie morning and for you to get up exactly at this time. He has your schedule all set out, and you are to make every effort to be timely."

The woman, who had yet to identify herself, had reached over and thrown the blankets back off her charge, which was met with a loud scream. Happy with the echoing sound of her own voice, she did it again. Once she completed a third shriek, the energetic woman decided she was having nothing of it.

She continued to reach into the bed, and Annalise could feel herself being pulled from the bed. In response, Annalise, the now angry bed occupant, pushed the invasive woman back, but other than getting a small reprieve, Annalise gained no ground. She quickly found herself rolled over on the bed, her bottom exposed, and loud smacking was the echo now heard produced by this woman's hand in the room attacking her sit upon.

She screamed, "Please, please, just stop," and when there didn't seem to be any end to the rhythmic pounding of the woman's large palm against her now swollen bottom, Annalise tried a different approach. Anna did what most children resorted to when the world did not appear to be responding in their favor. They called their rescuing parent. In this case, that was her papa that she yelled for by name. For every child knows, calling one's parent by their first name will get a quicker reply.

STEPHEN HAD BEEN IN his study, going over the books that had been somewhat neglected while he was in the city. He knew he had the first part of this morning free because Leesie would be learning about the routine when she was playing. He looked up when there was a rapping on his study door and when bade to enter it was his butler, Mr. Thorpe.

"Yes?" invited Stephen. "What is it? I am rather busy, as you can see."

Mr. Thorpe, in his very formal manner, said, "My lord, I believe there is a problem in your bedchamber with Lady Thayer."

Stephen leapt up from his chair and went towards the butler, gathering him out the door as he was walking out in the direction of his bedchamber. "What the devil could be wrong? I left her sleeping." Before the butler could respond, Stephen made it an unnecessary response. "I take it she having some difficulty reconciling this morning's schedule."

"Yes, my lord." The stoicism was profoundly marked by the lack of emotion.

Stephen sported a crooked grin that quickly left his face. "Yes, well, go about your business, Thorpe. I'll take care of it."

Stephen turned to take the steps in measured determination to stop the racket. Upon entering his bedchamber, he saw his wife lying across his bed and the woman he had hired to teach her what would be expected of her when she was Leesie pounding his bride's derrière intensely. The bottom in question was glowing red, with overlapping handprints beginning to swell and welt. The woman showed no signs of easing, and Stephen had no idea what his sprite could have done to call such retribution down on herself. In fact, he doubted she could do anything that horrendous.

Leesie's screams had stopped once Stephen reached the bottom of the staircase. The calling for Stephen or Papa had stopped as he was ascending, and all that was left was his little love softly moaning and shedding devastating tears. It wasn't a repentant cry, it wasn't an angry cry, it was an abandoned cry. A no hope cry that tore Stephen's heart so profoundly that when he saw the hand rhythmically raise in the preparation of another hand fall, his voice boomed across the room.

"That is enough!"

The sound of his words bounced off all matter in the room to re-assemble in the circular sphere about the three people in the center. The hand that was raised in preparation to fall once again stayed in its spot midair, and its owner's head wrenched to the left to lock eyes on her new employer. The description of those eyes could be nothing less than ferocious, dangerous, and Stephen hoped his thunderous look, together with his presence, spoke well for him. He also hoped the woman knew that should she make one more movement in the rhythm she had started, there was a great fear of her loss of abilities to do so ever again.

The room was silent except for the heart wrenching cries from his Leesie. Mrs. Mason, the woman who he had hired to protect and guide his most prized treasure, stood motionless after she eased her arm down to her side. Stephen noticed that the woman was heaving as if she had used great effort, but he tossed that aside as to be of no consequence.

He looked at his lovely Leesie and pushed the woman away, having no care for her person, as it didn't appear that she had any care for his precious wife. He climbed into the bed, leaned over and scooped up a still distraught wife, gathering her in his arms as he leaned them both against the head of the bed.

Turning to the woman, he said, "Leave us and gather your things." He stared until she left the room quite angrily, slamming the door behind her.

Leesie had yet to acknowledge his presence. She accepted his hold, but her crying was so profound. It wasn't that she was crying, for he expected to hear every type of cry that she would utter over the course of the years, but it was the quality of this cry. It was the cry of an abandoned child after they had realized they were abandoned. It was an unholy cry that he was fervently trying to abate, but finding no response thus far.

"Leesie, baby, listen to Papa. Listen to my voice. I've got you. You're okay. You're safe, darling. I'll protect you. I'll take care of you."

The devastation at hearing her cry almost paralyzed him once he had gotten the damn woman who he had trusted without more than a letter of reference with his Leesie. It seemed odd that his wife had not dropped out of her little role when she had found things not as they should be. Sometime he would ask her but now... now all he could do was rock her and hold her tight to himself and pray she'd forgive him.

He sat there cooing and cuddling for quite a while, waiting while she recovered. Until she acknowledged that her papa, or her husband, or bloody hell, even just Lord Thayer had her safe and secure, he continued comforting his darling all the while cursing the nanny and himself.

Finally, Leesie tried to speak, and after several false starts that immediately disintegrated into cries, she was successful. Her words came peppered with hiccups and stifled sobs.

"Oh, Papa, where were you? I cried and cried for you and you were gone. I thought that's what you wanted her to do to me. That you didn't love me."

"Shush, my love, you have to know me better than that." But she didn't. Why would she? He had broken trust with her already. "I would never want anyone to hurt you so terribly. Tell me why Mrs. Mason felt you needed to be chastised, and why so harshly?" Leesie shrugged and snuggled in closer.

"While I cannot agree with where the method went, I absolutely refuse to believe that this woman, who came highly recommended for these situations, decided to pummel your arse to the degree she obviously did, without provocation. And I expect the truth." There was no doubt of the sternness of his statement.

"I didn't want to get out of the bed."

"And?"

"That's all, Papa. I didn't want to get out of bed. I was still very tired." It was obvious that Leesie was feeling quite confident since it appeared her papa was on her side. He said he would always protect her from being hurt, such as that woman who had seared her flesh so efficiently.

"And?"

"And," Leesie began to pick the threads on the blanket covering her legs until her papa put his hand over hers. She looked up at him, and he raised his eyebrows, a very distinct response to her hesitancy. "And, well, I might have screamed."

"You might have screamed. However, since this is a past event, I believe you know exactly whether you screamed or did not. Do I need to assist in reigniting your bottom to get the full truth, or are you going to tell me? And be very aware that I will not ask again."

"Yes. I screamed. She tried to drag me out of bed, and I pushed her, but it didn't do anything, so I screamed. And then I screamed for you, but you didn't come."

"But I did come, I'm here."

"You didn't come when I screamed. You were not close enough to protect me. You came when I was so loud that it drew the maid. I sent her out to get help."

"Which maid?"

"Molly, the one you gave me to help me. I want her back. I don't want that lady."

It was quiet for a few moments as her hiccups ended. Her back stiffened, but she did not push out of his embrace.

"Stephen, I don't think I can be Leesie anymore. Leesie isn't able to stay safe, and I cannot risk harm again. I'm not sure I can trust you on that score. I had thought no one would know and sometimes, it calms me to be cuddled without the intimate gratification, but it's not worth this. Not ever."

Chapter 13

The comfort that was Leesie was gone away. Annalise was sitting in her husband's lap. She looked Stephen in the eyes and was very clear when she stated her response to him. It might have been his bride in his lap, but Lady Thayer who delivered the words.

"Stephen, you need to hear me. There are some things about being your little sprite that excite me. I like the lack of responsibility, at times. I like the fact that you will take care of me in a nurturing and loving way. I have needed that for so long, and the laughter. I love the giggles and the cuddles. It is truly healing." Her eyes looked at him, entreating his understanding, and he could do nothing but nod in his devastation that he knew he had created.

"I tolerated the bathing and some of the other things that you've mentioned, but the thing I will not do. I cannot allow is other people outside our senior staff to be privy to that part of our lives and certainly not to be treated in a harmful way." Annalise paused, taking a slow, steady breath. "That woman, no matter what her credentials and recommendations were, is not to interact with me on any level at any time ever again. If she does enter my room or my life ever again, I will walk out the door. I will hire myself out as whatever it is that I could hire myself out as, but I refuse to be treated so shamefully."

"I agree on Mrs. Mason, but not on any of the other. Do not be deceived into thinking I will ever let you go now that I have found you." He looked hard at his wife for a moment before gentling. "I should have alerted you to her hire, but I had no idea she would arrive until she did last evening. You were already asleep. Are you declining any nanny? Nannies can be wonderful for when you need to be Leesie, and I am unavailable to you."

"I don't need to be Leesie if you are not around. Know that it is you that draws me out in that way and only you that I will share that part of me with. I agreed to the Leesie part because I know it fills some part of me, but I never agreed to what I had today." She snuggled into her husband's chest, drawing more comfort before continuing. "What I experienced today did nothing towards building my trust or my level of security. Nothing good will come from anything that happened with that woman. I know as my husband you could force it, but I believe I would have a good enough reason to be able to leave without retribution. I have to know that you care enough about me to do this for me."

"Without any reservation, it shall never happen again. I believe after this morning's debacle, we shall have to recover our place of equilibrium again. I will resume teaching you tomorrow." Stephen stopped Annalise from speaking her objections. "Only if you will allow me. I will be your instructor for just two days a week. You will then practice those lessons for the following week, just as we had agreed. If you say no, then we will leave that part of our lives until you are ready to initiate it again."

"Does that mean that you will punish me?"

"Of course, but there are many ways to punish you, and they aren't always smacking bottoms. However, sometimes a way to release your stress will include smacking your bottom. You will need to submit to whatever the punishment is, for I promise to be judicious in dealing it out."

"Stephen, am I to be punished in all areas of our life?"

Stephen laughed. "Oh, my dear, discipline will be in all areas of your life. For little sprites, there are little sprite chastisements, for grand ladies there are grand lady reprimands, and for the wanton woman in my bed, there are even different penalties. Have no fear that the person and the crime shall match and ne'er the twain shall meet amongst other roles in your life."

"Might I have some breakfast now?" Stephen laughed and lightly patted her bottom to her accompanying squeal.

"Papa, that hurts," said a satisfied and ready to play Leesie.

"So, I am Papa again? Have I satisfied you enough so soon?"

"Not entirely, but I did love the times we played. And I loved them most because you allowed me to decide. This morning was nothing about me. I don't know who it was about, but I think we agree it wasn't either of us, really."

"Yes, well, I need to go and take care of discharging Mrs. Mason. I need to explain to her that her services, or her extreme brand of services, are not required. Nevertheless, you do understand when you are ready to play again, my dear, we commence. While I agree that she is not the right woman for us, if you take me on as a taskmaster in this area, I will be very exacting and you are expected to follow me implicitly. Have no question on that score." He pulled her into his chest again, tipping her face up to him. "Now, are you Leesie or Annalise?"

"Annalise. I am soured on play today."

"Good, then I am in the right frame of mind," he said as he leaned down to kiss her lips. "It's too late to have a tray into your room, so let me bring you downstairs and alert the kitchen that you shall need breakfast in the dining room. When I am through with my business, I will assist you. I'll send your maid in to help you."

"But no references."

"I hardly can give her reference, but I can give her back her old reference, once I take down the name of the writer of the same."

"Very well, but do you have to contact him? I mean, won't he ask questions about children and so on?"

"No dear, this was the reference from a group of friends I have who are very familiar with this type of play. I shall simply inquire as to his reasoning."

"Very well then."

The rest of the morning was spent in recovery for Annalise, discharging Mrs. Mason, and sending a letter of inquiry to the writer of the reference. After lunch, it was the agreed time for her lessons as Lady Thayer. For those lessons, he employed Mrs. Thorpe to add to her daily responsibilities until such time as Annalise had enough understanding to need only a little instruction.

Lord Thayer felt it wouldn't be that long, but until then Mrs. Thorpe gladly took on the responsibility of training the Lady Thayer for the running of her home. Stephen would compensate her as he would any other tutor.

The next day, the start of her morning was considerably different. Stephen had gotten up, dressed and went down to start his morning allowing Annalise to sleep in knowing that once he woke her up, she was to be Leesie until midday. Determined to avoid the same type of rude awakening as the day before, Stephen laid a plan to ensure a gentler start to the morning.

He spoke with Molly, the helpful maid, and found out that his bride might not be a jump up out of bed morning person so he felt a more easing into the new day would work for her. Their mornings, until yesterday, were leisurely, typically unscheduled and accomplished together. With that in mind, he helped her get up slowly by rousing her after he had gone down and had his breakfast, never one to take a tray in bed.

He sent Molly up to roust her again, with a tray of muffin and cocoa. He then went to attend to some early-morning details on the estate. He came back upstairs, followed by Molly, who seemed to have assigned herself to Annalise. He wondered if he shouldn't suggest she become official. His wife needed an abigail. He would talk to Mrs.

Thorpe. He encouraged the maid to help her mistress dress, which she did so demurely.

There was a little bit of petulance when Leesie did not want to wear the dress that was chosen for her, but her papa settled that quickly.

"Leesie, I have yet to decide what age I believe you are. If you cannot behave at an appropriate age to be able to choose your clothing with minimal assistance, then you shall have no input at all. For now, it is my choice. Show me you are ready for that task and I shall give it back. Do you understand?"

"Yes, Papa, but I did not choose my gown. I should have rather chosen the lavender one." Annalise sighed in resignation. She then turned to Molly and said, "I shall wear the blue one." She turned and looked at her papa displaying a little of the original spark that first drew him to her when she said, "Even if I've already worn a blue dress this week." And she turned to put her arms up to have the gown brought over her head.

Stephen was finding that the indulgent part of him was forever appearing with this little sprite. So she liked to wear different colors. He would try to remember that. My, how he loved her so. His mother was missing out on a daughter that had sparkle, and vivaciousness supported by such a strong backbone that even the marchioness would have had to approve if only she would acquiesce that he could make his own marriage partner choices.

He had proven he was able to do so, even if she did not agree. It was like allowing Leesie the option of being able to pick her own gown, demonstrate the ability to be mature enough. He was an accomplished businessman, and yet she felt she was still wiser than he was. She would come around, but all the time she lost would never be able to be recovered.

The afternoon came, and Mrs. Thorpe was excellent at what she did and was a thorough but kind tutor. She began at the beginning.

She explained about creating, receiving and turning away guests. She progressed to tableware setting and usage, followed by seating arrangements. They spoke of what the duties of Lady Thayer were to the household, to her husband, to the community, and Annalise herself. Her ladyship was quite enthralled with all that it entailed.

"Now milady, we must discuss that there are things such as the annual event that the estate house hosts."

"Oh? That sounds rather fun. Tell me about it."

"It is put on for all those who are dependent upon the property for their welfare as well as the village at large. Since you are here now, you will be doing so in conjunction with Marchioness Thayer and your sister-in-law."

"But his lordship's mother doesn't like me. How am I to work with her?"

"His lordship will make it happen, don't you worry. It is months away, yet."

Annalise watched as the frustrating moments of the day were met by Mrs. Thorpe briskly. She let nothing ruffle her feathers and, therefore, very effectively taught Lady Thayer how to handle things without too much drama. Mrs. Thorpe was very clear that Lord Thayer was not a man who put up with drama.

"You need to heed my words, my dear. I have become rather fond of you already. Will you allow me to speak freely?"

"Always speak freely with me when it is appropriate. I owe so much to you, and I trust your judgment."

"Well then, milady, trust these words. I have never seen his lordship so focused on one person as he is with you. He does have his peculiarities, which I am sure you have figured out but if you can find your way clear to learn him, and love him as he is, I believe you will find what you are looking for. He will help you find a purpose and place you can share with your children and their children. You will always be protected in the shelter of his arms."

"But shouldn't he also trust me?"

"I am sure he does. The first taste of trust is automatic, my dear, but remember that once that trust is tainted, it is work to earn it back."

Chapter 14

Several days later, Leesie had been instructed to read a book on history, which she did under protest. "It is recent history and still under discussion in drawing rooms across England."

It was a torment. It was a history of the monarchy and expansion to the Americas, neither of which Leesie cared about at all. She'd been reading for approximately forty minutes and had run out of drawings in the book. She tried to read the book, but it was such a dry and uninteresting topic that it just got worse and worse. The descriptions were not easy for her to comprehend, for her reading ability was adequate but not overly stunning. She took the book and was going to rip out several of the pages in her frustration but knew that her papa would be quite angry at that response.

Instead, she simply chucked the whole at the fireplace. She missed the fire but hit the mantle, knocking over a candelabrum. It came crashing to the ground with a great clanging, candles rolling across the floor in a seemingly mad dash to reach the other end of the room.

Still irritated that she was made to read such things, she left the mess where it was and went for a walk in the garden, leaving one of the doors open for she intended to use it to reenter the library. Her intention was to go back and pick things up, but she was supposed to have time with her papa today, and because he was busy, he had made her read those horrid books.

Papa had gone to do Lord Thayer business, and so when he returned home, the events of the day were recounted to him by Mr.

Thorpe. And then they were recounted once again by a repentant little girl when the maid was sent for his wife. Leesie arrived in answer
to his request. As she entered the study after knocking, he instructed
her to close and lock the door. After hesitating, she did so. The look
on her papa's face was suppressed anger that she had experienced on
several occasions. She knew no good would come of it if she turned
tail and ran, so she decided to stay and endure the results of her actions.

Leesie had never been called to his study before and was feeling
quite contrite by the time she had stood in front of his desk. She had
come back from wandering the garden when she discovered both
doors open to the library and smoke rolling out. She rushed in to
find out what the commotion was about and saw the book she had
thrown, doused with water and melted candles on the carpeted floor
near it. The rest of the room appeared untouched except for the
smoke that seemed to have settled on the wooden walls, the books,
the shelves, tables, and chairs.

Looking at her papa, she quickly looked away, for his demeanor
made her quake in her button up shoes. She ran the toe of her shoes
along the floor and whispered, still looking down.

"Did I do all that damage, Papa?" She instinctively put her hands
behind her to cover her bottom. She was sure it would feel his anger
momentarily.

"You tell me, young lady. How is it that you were instructed to sit
in the library and read a book that I gave you until such time as you
were released from that obligation and yet could not be found soon
after?"

"I read for forty minutes."

"Really? I see I stand corrected."

Somehow, she knew it was a bad choice to correct him at this
precise moment.

"How is it that long before you were released, the room was found full of smoke, candle wax on the floor, a smoldering book, and the garden door open but no inhabitant?"

His questions were delivered calmly, in a very even voice that unnerved Leesie more than if he were raging. She sniffled and tears clogged her throat as the full realization of her actions brought down her shame. Her chin began to tremble, and her teeth began to bite into her lower lip.

"Leesie, I need you to answer me."

In a voice that caught on every syllable, she responded, "It was my fault, Papa. I was upset that I had to read about things that I didn't understand well, and it was confusing. I was angry that because I couldn't read faster, or better, that I couldn't go out into the garden."

"And then what did you do?"

"I threw the book, and it hit the candelabra, and I left everything everywhere. I didn't see that it touched the fire, honestly. I went out into the garden. I'm so sorry, I'm so sorry. Please, I'm sorry, don't send me away." Her words came out in a rush, and her tears flowed fast and free as a waterfall.

Stephen was trying to make sense of the jumble of words his contrite miss was saying, and just as he was catching up to what had happened, he was shocked to hear her fear of being sent away. There she was, standing on the other side of his desk in abject fear and shame twice in recent history, crying the sorrow of desertion. It was more than he could handle. He knew he needed to discipline her for her act, but for the moment, all he could do was comfort her and reassure her that under no conditions would he send her away. He already loved her too much.

He quickly stood and rounded his desk to gather her in his arms, holding and cuddling her as she continued to cry without ceasing. He gathered her up in his arms and carried her to the sofa, cooing and trying to calm her down. She began speaking, but he didn't understand what she was saying, and as he would shush her so that she would calm down, she became more excited with her effort to speak.

Finally, she was able to slow her crying just enough, so that words were more intelligible coming out of her mouth. She grabbed onto Stephen's shirt tightly and tried to anchor herself into a steadier voice until ultimately she spoke, taking deep breaths before uttering her words.

"Papa," she hiccupped, "you have to spank me. I feel so wretched. I'm horrible. You have to spank me hard."

"No, no, we will talk about that later. Papa just wants you to calm down and understand I'm not going to ever send you away. It was not a good thing to do, and we will address that soon, but please, you must believe me. There is nothing in this world that would convince me to send you away. Hush, sweetheart, I love you. I would never send you from my sight. I would be devastated if you were gone."

"But I was horrid. You have to. I'm so guilty. I feel so rotten; I'm never going to feel good again. Please, please, you have to help me be good again. You have to help me be clean again."

She started to rock back and forth, her sobs taking back over. Whatever else she mumbled, he couldn't quite understand, but he'd understood enough. Her guilt was overtaking her, and if she didn't calm down, she would soon be sick. As her papa, he must do what she needed to make her feel good again. As her husband, he also had no doubt that something else was going on. Something else was behind this desperate outburst, a memory perhaps from her childhood.

This wasn't about him being angry, this wasn't even about all the soot in the room, and it wasn't about her disobedience. This was about her redemption. She couldn't ask for it as his Anna or Annalise because that is not who caused the problem. She could not accept the retribution as Lady Thayer because she did not cause the problem. She must accept it as Leesie because she was the one who was naughty.

"Leesie, listen to me. You are right, this was a terribly naughty thing to do, and you're going to be disciplined. Papa is going to correct the naughty behavior now, but remember, I love you and if you need something else or to talk about something else, you can tell me."

He stood her up to his right side, moving both of them so that he was in the middle of the sofa. He pulled down the pillow so that it would support her. He knew this had to be a cleansing spanking as well as a discipline one, so she would need something to hold onto. Squeezing the pillow would help her muffle her cries and draw comfort.

There was no lecture. There was no warmup. Stephen pushed up her gown, throwing the layers over her head, further muffling her sounds. Without any more preamble, he brought down his hand in merciless strength. He had to steel his sensibilities to her cries, for their source was tangled. He spanked hard and fast. One, two, three, switch sides, one, two, and three. Repeatedly he swatted and carefully waited for the release, but none came.

Her bottom went from pink to red to deep crimson and still no flood of cleansing tears. He peppered her upper thighs and the underside of her cheeks, to no avail. There wasn't anything else he could do but to send her up to her room with a kiss and another reassurance that she was his forever. Stephen was broken-hearted. He condemned himself for making her read a book she was not interested in. While he didn't cause the accident, he could have avoided it happening.

It was late in the day by the time the library was discovered and, therefore, not a thorough cleaning was accomplished. The rest would need to be completed the next day. While it was typical for Annalise to have dinner with Stephen, she refused to leave her room. Her husband understood that this was still a difficult transition time for her.

His wife needed to work out that what Leesie did would not shine a detrimental night on Lady Thayer or Annalise. He had a much better understanding of her needs as Leesie than she did herself. It would come in time.

He had no misconceptions as to why his bride was able to be Leesie. He understood the need to be nurtured as a child and all through life, but without those beginning pieces of structure and ever-growing responsibility and unfettered love, you miss them the rest of your life. He didn't know about others, but his darling had missed some important years with a father who loved her. Unfortunately, as an adult, it was nearly impossible to get those things satisfied outside of play like this. This was a way to cleanse and heal for her.

He had always been a nurturer. When he asked himself why it was so important to allow her to have that emotional deficit filled in this way, he just knew that it gave him joy to allow her to be that little girl when she needed to be. He had discovered this about himself when he was a young man of sixteen and his cousin, who was now married to one of his good friends, had demonstrated her need to be allowed time as a little girl. After she had married his friend, Stephen had had long conversations with Bertram. He was able to answer all the questions Stephen had about that growing need in him to nurture a woman with those requirements.

That was when his search to find the woman who would fill that need for him with that desire, known or unknown to the woman, until Annalise came into his life. He recognized it immediately, and while her station in life had been no station at all, that didn't matter. What mattered was that she had wants and needs that he could fill, thereby satisfying his own internal cravings.

This evening, when he learned that she had thrown the book, knocked the candelabra, and stormed out of the library, he knew she was missing something that was hidden inside. She was too devastated for such a disaster over smoke. It was too heated, too aggressive not to hold another meaning. He tried not to discipline her often and was rather successful at that, but structure was something he also lacked in when it came to Leesie. That lack of security and an unreliable schedule produced this error that he would not make again.

While chastising her for her temper was not something that he enjoyed, he now understood it was a part of her needs, which he had not fully met. He believed this was his fault for not strengthening the boundaries with which she could walk. He would not make that mistake again. To that end, he made sure that the punishment she had received this evening was dramatic, no matter how difficult it was for him to deliver.

And by her response, dramatic was most needed.

While he'd hoped she would feel cleansed by his thrashing, evidently she felt the need for more. Therefore, when she indicated that need by refusing to leave her bedroom, he allowed her to stay. He thought over the conversation they had had in her bedroom just prior to dinner.

"My dear, it's time for dinner. You've not dressed? Annalise the meal will be ready to serve in ten minutes. You shall have to go down in what you have on, and there will be a price to pay for not following the rules. I don't know what's gotten into you, but we will figure it out."

"I'm not going down to eat. I'm not hungry."

Her peevish behavior was his first sign that things were not set to right yet. He decided to explore.

"Annalise, your husband requires your presence at his dining table. Now." His voice left no doubt that he was serious and intended that she follow his command.

"I won't." She snapped as her foot came crashing to the floor, highlighting her irritability.

He noted her behavior did not snap her out of her Leesie persona as it sometimes did. He decided to try one last time in hopes that he would dine with his wife tonight.

"Annalise, I have things to speak to you about this evening. I would like to do so over dinner. Come, my dear."

Stephen held his arm out to receive her hand and watched, chagrined, when she again stomped her foot. He sighed but knew that he needed to change tactics. His desires were not going to supersede her own this evening. She was stuck in her need to be Leesie, and they would have to deal with it before she could move on. Her next statement sealed the evening.

"Papa, please don't make me. My bottom hurts. And my heart is sad." Her shoulders slumped as she clasped her hands in front of her and looked at the floor.

"Yes, my sprite, I can see that today has not been a good day for you and staying in your room will be the best thing. However," the gentleness easing out of his voice and the sternness taking its place, "you will eat. I will have Molly bring you a tray, but if you do not eat what's on your tray, I will be quite annoyed. I will come back up here, and your heart will be even sadder because your bottom will hurt even more. Am I understood?" His stance was fully paternal, and her response was fully juvenile. And he was completely confused.

"Yes, Papa."

Chapter 15

Stephen had dinner alone and was devastated and lonely. He accepted this as one of those times that her needs were going to be outside of his desires and he would always meet his wife's requirements first. That didn't mean that he enjoyed his time alone, for he'd had plenty of years of that.

After dinner, he went up to check on his little sprite. He was surprised to find that Leesie had eaten half of her food and left the other half on the plate. She was dressed in her nightgown and was sitting on her bed as though waiting for him to return. When he walked in the door, she looked up with still very sad eyes. He was stumped. He'd done everything that she wanted him to do. He'd spanked her harder than he was comfortable, allowed her to stay little, sent her a meal to her, and still, it didn't seem to lighten her heart. There was something else wrong.

He solemnly sat on her bed. "Does Leesie want to sleep in her bed or does Annalise want to sleep in my bed?"

He intended on giving her the choice, although he preferred to simply take over and have things in its proper routine. He definitely was a man of schedule, and while it was out of character for his wife, it was certainly out of his comfort zone to be off his routine. He had never realized that so much as when he became a husband and habitual practices shifted to accommodate his wife. He didn't mind the adjustments, however, once it was set, any disturbance caused discord to his own constitution.

"Stay here, please. This is where Leesie should sleep. Leesie doesn't sleep with Papa." Her voice was very timid, and he could hear the shame, self-depreciation, and great regression in her conversation. Right now she was small, six or seven at the oldest.

"Quite so. Leesie plays with her papa, but she doesn't sleep with him. Sweetheart, are you sure? You've never slept alone."

"Yes, I know, but it will be fine. I shall be very brave."

Stephen let that go. Picking up his papa persona smoothly, he turned his attention to her half-consumed plate of food.

"I believe you were to eat the food served to you."

"Yes." She looked down at the covering and traced the pattern of the embroidery.

"And yet I still see a considerable amount of food left on your plate. You did not follow my instructions. Can you tell Papa why?"

Leesie looked up and shrugged her shoulders, still with a sad countenance. "I don't know if I actually deserve it. But I was quite hungry after I took the first bite, so I ate some. I know that was selfish and I know I should have stuck to nothing, but I just couldn't."

She was breaking his heart. She was also manipulating the outcome of punishment. He needed her to understand that he knew what she was doing and that it wasn't her place to decide penances. It was his place as her papa.

"Leesie," he said sternly after drawing her into his lap. He suspected that he knew what she needed and he would try to give it to her.

"Papa told you to eat everything on your tray. You have chosen not to. If I had wanted you to go without food, I would have said so. I will never say that. There are sweets you might be denied, and there are many things I might deny you in pleasure, but never food for nourishment. I don't know why you are still intent on punishing yourself, but that is wrong since that is not your job. Somehow, you still feel the need for chastisement, but I choose when you need discipline, not you. I shall respond to your needs as I choose."

Leesie was nodding her head and slow hot tears overflowing the banks of her eyes, sliding down the mounds of her cheeks. He sat her back on her bottom on the bed, getting up himself and walking towards the tray. He gathered it up and brought it back to the bed, setting it down.

"I want you to open your mouth and let me feed you."

Her eyes were wide with unbelief. "Feed me?"

"Yes, feed you. You may never decide you have no worth. I forbid it, and I will prove it by feeding you myself. Now open up."

She opened her mouth like a little bird and ate every bite. He gave her water from her tray, and she drank it down.

"Now, you will receive another spanking because you tried to manipulate me into punishment." Her eyes grew wide. "I shall be right back, young lady. You need to prepare yourself."

He could see the response to his words and was satisfied that it was in the direction that she felt she needed, even if he didn't agree. When he returned, she had indeed done as he requested, her still pink but not red bottom on display across the bed. To his relief, there was not a sign of bruising.

He saw her body tense when he opened their adjoining door and then saw her shift as she heard the snap of the lock first one, then the other entrance. He loudly unwrapped brown paper that he had acquired on the day he married his little sprite. The riding crop and another implement, the tawse, lay where she could see them on the bed.

He could hear the alarm in her voice when she saw the implements. "Oh, Papa, what are those? You are not going to, I mean, those are not for my bottom, are they?"

Her distress was real, and since she felt her accident today was almost unforgivable, he felt that she needed to feel the wrath of something stronger than his hand. He had no intentions of it being a hard administration. However, the fact that he was using an implement rather than his bare hand should do the trick. It should make her feel absolved of all guilt. At least he prayed it did.

"Oh yes. I love you very much, and if your naughty little bottom gets into great mischief, it needs a greater chastisement. I have no doubt that you will feel these strokes more than my hand. I believe the lesson will have been learned and the guilty slate clean after this."

He chose his words well because he did not want her to believe that there would be any guilt left after this session. He wanted his joyful Leesie back. And his cock wanted Anna back, and his household needed Lady Thayer back. But most importantly, husband and wife needed Annalise back, the woman who embodied all things in his world. When Annalise was happy, then his world would be happy again.

He made a great show of raising the tawse after positioning her just so. He wanted to soothe her fears but knew that it was those exact trepidations that would help accomplish the deed tonight. He raised his hand and brought the tawse to a snapping bite on her presented bottom that she immediately tried to cover with her hands. He had prepared for that and brought back with him several scarves.

"Papa can tie your hands because they cannot come back during your punishment or you will be hurt."

She did not resist him when he laid down the tawse near her face and firmly tied her hands together. He picked up the tawse and placed it on her back, only to reach over and position her bottom higher with pillows under her belly, creating a better target.

He then picked up the riding crop, the other implement in the brown paper wrapping and moved it through the air several times so that she could hear the sound of it swishing through the air, further heightening her apprehension and assisting him in his cause. He struck her presented bottom at the fleshy part. He repeated it three times, enough to bite, but nothing more. His little sprite was already sobbing, but he was confident that he was not striking her hard, for the lines were only light.

Laying down the crop, he grabbed the tawse again. "Okay, sweetheart, ten with this and we will be done."

She nodded her head, but he didn't require her to answer, for her sobs were still too much to allow a discernible word to be uttered. The tawse snapped again, leaving stinging stripes over the stripes left by the crop reigniting the burning that had begun to subside from those lines. At every touch of the lash, light though it was, she jumped until the last two produced a response that was a moan.

He didn't know if the moaning was from the arousal of her womanly charms or exhaustion from her little girl chastisement. Regardless he leaned down after the last stroke, to run his hand over her dark pink but not red bottom making sure that he had not misjudged any of his strokes and was glad to see he had not.

He patted her bottom as he spoke. "All right, my little sprite, let's put you to rights and get you under your cover on your tummy. You won't be comfortable to sleep any other way this evening, but I think it's been such a long day it will be easy for you to rest. I'll take your tray out with me. Do you need the chamber pot?"

"No thank you, Papa."

Her voice sounded groggy but not so sad, and he hoped that this would remedy her feelings of guilt. He would have to find another method if it didn't, for he was not going to stripe her again. The torture to himself was too great, and he knew a little bottom that needed healing.

Stephen awoke to a rapping on his door and an insistent, "My lord, my lord."

"Yes, yes, open the door. Who is it?" he demanded testily. He had not had a good night's sleep thus far and did not take well to the interruption during the period of time he was actually sleeping.

Stephen tried to clear the sleep from his eyes and the fogginess from his brain. He looked up to focus on Mr. Thorpe, his butler. Nothing could be good if Mr. Thorpe was at his door.

"What the devil is wrong, man?"

"My lord, it's Lady Thayer."

"Lady Thayer?" Stephen sat up quickly in alarm. "What is it, man? Speak up. What's the matter with Lady Thayer? Is she hurt? Ill?"

"No, sir, she is not hurt. But I don't know what is wrong, except she's in the library."

"The library? I thought it wasn't cleaned yet."

"It hadn't been completed, but Lady Thayer is in there, cleaning it."

It was apparent to Stephen that Mr. Thorpe had absolutely no idea what to do with that information. He'd never seen the lady of the house clean anything prior to this in all of his years as a butler. As Stephen sat there for a moment processing the information, he shook his head before a slight smile touched his lips. He got out of bed and put on his robe and slippers, growling at the cold room.

He patted Mr. Thorpe on the back, then sent him back to his room.

"I'll take care of Lady Thayer. Please do not disclose what you have seen here tonight, Thorpe. I know it seems odd, but all will be well, and Lady Thayer will be mortified if she thought anyone had observed her."

Mr. Thorpe could be relied on to adhere to a strict set of rules governing his position. He could be trusted to follow those instructions to the letter, which included no gossip.

As Stephen approached the library door, he listened to see if he could hear anything in the room, but the walls and the doors were too thick. He entered the room and what he saw answered his questions. His lovely wife was on the ground, in a full apron, long honey hair flowing as she scrubbed a spot on the carpet. She was so hard at work she didn't notice that he was in the room just as she had not noticed that Mr. Thorpe was in the room earlier.

After standing for a moment watching her run a rag over the carpet, he interrupted her activity by clearing his throat. Annalise brought her head up with a snap and stared at her husband in the same way that deer stared at torch fire when hunting them.

"Annalise, sweetheart, what are you doing?"

"Oh, you frightened me, Stephen."

Her voice was stronger than it had been earlier in the evening and he could hear the slight reproach. It made his heart dance. It meant his wife was coming back again and whatever it was that was torturing her was beginning to leave. He hoped that at this moment, in this transitional place, he could find out why she was so tortured so that they could avoid it again. He waited until she continued.

"I believe that is self-evident. I'm trying to rid the room of the soot that I put in it." She dropped a scrubbing rag into the bucket of murky water that she had and put her hands on her apron-covered hips, staring at her husband.

"Annalise, that's why we employ servants, sweetheart. They earn their money by doing things such as this. You don't want to take away a person's livelihood so that we don't need them anymore and must let them go, surely."

"Do not tease me, my lord. It has indeed been a long day."

"It has indeed. And a longer night if the evidence before me speaks true," he responded.

"Yes, it has been a rather long night."

He could hear that her voice was lighter, and she had been able to laugh. He knew that thankfully, they were almost through this incident. His curiosity and his need to know was too great to let it drop, however.

"And this," he gestured with a sweep of his hand, "is because of your guilt." It was a statement of fact.

Annalise ducked her head down for a moment before lifting it up and looking at her husband straight on. "Yes."

"Please leave that for even a moment while we go into the front parlor. I have to ask you some questions, and this room is cold, however I'm sure there's still a fire going in one of the common rooms."

He reached his hand out and waited for her to cross the floor and put her hand in his. He turned her around and helped remove the apron. He then grabbed her hand again and led her out of the room, quietly closing the door behind them. In the parlor, he drew her to a sofa and sat down.

"Now, I'm going to speak, and then you are going to speak." That was not a request, it was once again a statement of fact. The nodding of her head was all that was required.

"I need to recap the incident today as I understand it, so that I'm sure I know what was going on. It is paramount that we are honest with each other, but I feel that either you were unable to be entirely truthful with me or it was possible that you weren't quite sure what was going on yourself. So let me begin by saying I absolutely love the interactions that we have when you are Leesie. It fulfills me in a way that nothing else ever could, and I now believe it satisfies you in a similar way."

Annalise nodded her head. She opened her mouth to explain, but he stayed her with his hand and a shake of his head. He continued.

"But I am at a loss as to the full extent of the events this afternoon. And so as I understand it, you were angry that you were instructed to read, something you don't care to do often. And I chose a rather challenging book on your patience, for which I will try not to do again. Nonetheless, the incident happened, and then you were chastised for it. That should have been the end of the episode. However, it wasn't. It was as though you were stuck because something was preventing you from changing roles. It was as though you felt you did not deserve to leave the punishment of your acts today."

He looked at her again, waiting for her to either agree or disagree. She nodded her head again in agreement. He continued.

"And so I tried to accommodate that need for further chastisement because you couldn't let the incident go and you forced me to discipline you again." He waited for her to further agreed which she did.

"And finally, when I felt that a mere Papa spanking was not going to cleanse your guilt, I brought out the crop and the tawse. That should have been enough and yet here you are in the library, in the middle of the night, cleaning it like a common maid whose job it is to set the room to rights. So, something else is going on here, and I need to hear it. You need to tell it to me. We need to get rid of it."

Chapter 16

Stephen sat back in his seat to indicate that he was through speaking and that it was now her turn. Annalise sat for just a moment before she spoke. She took a deep breath, blew it out, and looked into her husband's eyes, that were gentle and compassionate. And confused. She knew it was time to tell what had been bothering her all afternoon and evening. She hadn't known it herself until later this evening.

"You're right." Her voice was robust, having left the little girl tucked away for when she needed her again.

"When I was a very young child, probably about six or nearly seven years old because that's the last time that my father was home, a terrible thing happened. Something I cannot change, but it made such a difference in my mother's life and apparently mine." She took a staggered breath and slowly let it out before continuing.

"My father was called to go to His Majesty's navy to fight Napoleon. Only he didn't go in that direction. They placed him on a ship towards the Americas, the colonies. Because they were also waging war, I guess. It seems that Britain is always fighting somebody. But anyway, I was a little girl who didn't want her daddy to leave." Annalise went to stand. Stephen reached over to stay her but thought better of it and removed his hand, allowing her to walk the room as she spoke.

"So it was the day that he was to leave again, and my parents had spent the last few days together. I was only able to play with him for short periods of time. I'm sure it was for longer than I realized, but to me, at that age, it was just a few moments. Just snatches of time and it appeared that my mother had all of my father's time." Her agitation began to rise again, and just as Stephen was about to go to her, she seemed to rein in her emotions enough to continue.

"And so the day came that he was to leave. And when we were saying goodbye, he told me that he would be back and to take care of my mother. Of course, that's a ridiculous thing to say to a six-year-old, but he thought that would make me behave, I suppose." She rounded the room a full rotation, arms wrapped around her middle in a daydream only she was in before she continued.

"And he said that if anything were to happen, he would be right back to take care of us. He left, and my mother cried and I with her for a number of days. Until finally she seemed to have decided she had cried enough and we created a routine of sorts. But I never forgot that he said if anything were to happen, he would be right back. And to a little girl, that was a promise she expected her daddy to keep."

Tears began to roll down her cheeks, and she angrily brushed them away. She no longer took glances over in the direction of Stephen. She had stopped at the doors leading to the garden and just stood looking into the darkness.

"I thought if I did something, not horrible but scary, somehow he would know that we needed him and he would come back." She paused again and then continued. "In our small sitting room, in the front of the fireplace, I started a fire by carrying a stick from the parlor fire into the sitting room, and I added all sorts of things I knew would burn, kindling, straw, cloth, and books. The problem was, no one went in for quite a while. And because it wasn't near the front of the house, and it had been dusted in the morning, it took quite a while for anyone to realize that there was a fire."

"Oh, darling." Stephen stood and placed his hand on her shoulder. She jumped and jerked away from him as though his hand were leprous.

"Being a small child who forgets things quickly when presented with a distraction, I went out to play. I don't really know everything that happened after that. I remember there was some smoke coming out of the window, people rushing around, putting me in the kitchen, crying and yelling. Cook gave me something to eat to keep me occupied, I guess, but I was beginning to get scared. Finally, my mother came to me and explained that one of the young housemaids that we had was gone."

She appeared to have come out of her daze of storytelling, her voice now brisk and businesslike. She was now just recounting something as though she had read or heard about it.

"It was much later that evening that I found out what had happened. Because the fire was in the front, not inside the fireplace proper, its flames burned things it normally would not have done, like the mantelpiece. The maid had gone to investigate and opened the door.

"She went inside, unfortunately. When she approached the fireplace, the mantle, which was huge, fell on her, catching her clothing on fire. Her screams brought other people to the room, but by that time, she was too badly burned. She did not survive. And the smell of burnt flesh will never be out of my memory."

Annalise looked Stephen firmly in the eye and said, "and of course, by that time my father was already dead, and he couldn't have come back even were it possible, which it would not have been."

"And now I see why you could not accept a mere punishment and forgiveness in this."

"Yes. You see, when this happened today, because of irresponsibility on my part, I could smell burnt flesh, and I could hear the yelling. I was in the house of my early childhood again. I was a little girl again. I never told a soul that I started the fire in a juvenile attempt to bring my father home. In fact, it had left my daily memory some time ago. Consequently, when this happened, it brought back all the horror and the pain and the massive guilt that I still had for the other event. I still have it now. And so I needed to scrub the room myself. I didn't want anyone else to do it."

"At some juncture, you're going to have to let it go. It will rule your life otherwise. What will it take for you to feel absolved of the crime you believe you committed but that surely cannot be laid at the feet of a small child?"

"Allow me to complete the cleaning of the room. Let me clean the entire room. Whatever is left that I can clean. I don't know if it will take away the guilt, but it is undoing as much as I can undo." She looked up at her husband with pleading eyes, begging him to understand.

"May I do it with you?" It was such an innocent question, and yet it filled that last little piece that she needed to fully trust him in all things. No matter how horrible a thing that had happened in her past, he would stand with her. She knew she loved him at that moment. He was doing what she had hoped in her young heart her own father would do. Come and save the day.

"Yes, of course."

She didn't say what they both knew. He could have forbidden her. He could have told her that it wasn't her place. That she was the matron of the house and was not allowed to do menial labor. He could tell her he would have nothing to do with it and go back to bed. He could've condemned her for disclosing her memory and a small child who unwittingly had caused such a great tragedy.

But he did none of those things. He accepted her memories as they were and accepted what his wife felt she needed to do to right those wrongs. He did it with her. She needed his acceptance and his love. That's what he offered. Together, they cleaned the library the best they would be able to do alone.

"May I take my wife to bed now?" Stephen asked quietly.

"Oh yes, please."

Annalise would not need to mention the incident again, but knew it sealed that last crack in their newly laid foundation. She could trust Lord Stephen Thayer with her deepest needs and he would walk that road with her. He was everything she would ever need.

As the weeks progressed, Annalise began to understand even more deeply her need to have separate roles but that she not acknowledge them as individual entities for they were all her. It allowed her to flow seamlessly from one role to another without fanfare. Just as she was a daughter, wife, and niece, and hopefully one day a mother, all with unique expectations, she was also Leesie and the lady of the house with various tasks and expectations. Her needs that she had never acknowledged were being met on such a deep level that when she sat to think about it all, it was quite profound.

On certain days, training or the lessons she was learning in whatever realm of life they belonged to were daunting. Stephen had left off the Leesie training, for he said he learned from her, but that persona had the most pitfalls. In reality, there were many other areas of learning that she must participate in. When overwhelmed, her temper would appear, and as Mrs. Thorpe had advised, Lord Thayer did not like drama. She had learned that he also had a distaste for his daily schedule to be disrupted due to that drama. It was on those days that she was most likely to find herself learning new discipline methods at her husband's hand. Today had been a tough day.

"What is that confounded slamming of doors?" His lordship demanded after the third one sounded.

"I believe it has to do with a young lady and music lessons, my lord."

Stephen had employed a lady's tutor, Miss Bell, whom he had very carefully vetted. She was a godsend and Annalise was benefiting. His darling, however, could be stubborn.

Stephen looked at his clock with exasperation. Some days his countess was quite taxing on the patience. He stood and briskly walked to the music room, finding it empty but sheet music scattered on the floor. The new timing machine, the metronome that Stephen was offered to sample for usefulness at home, was still keeping time, now to nothing but silence. Walking back to his study to resume his work, he left instructions that when his wife was located, to send her and her tutor to his study.

Stephen had just completed his review of the weekly totals when there was a solid knock on the door. Putting aside his work, Stephen called permission to enter and watched with amusement as his wife, in all her glory, walked into the room led by Thorpe who stood just inside the room and Miss Bell directly behind her. Having now been able to see the emotional changes in his wife, he saw her worry, for she was concentrating on her feet as she walked. Stephen stood to receive them.

"Thank you, Thorpe. That is all." Turning to the tutor, he asked, "Miss Bell, how is our day going thus far?"

"Well, Lord Thayer, it has not gone as well as most days."

"I see, and do you know the reason for that?"

"Of course, not all days are going to be as productive as others. I believe it is just an off day, milord."

"And who is feeling off? Is it you or my wife?"

"It may be both of us, milord."

"Hmm. Have you been back to the music room since Leesie stormed out?"

"Oh, I wasn't teaching Leesie today, milord. I was teaching her ladyship. And no, we have not. We were directed to come straightaway to your study."

"Thank you. What have you not done today that you normally do?"

"We have done everything, except finish the music lesson, milord."

"Very well, then I release you for the rest of the day to do as you desire."

"Thank you, and I would remind your lordship that I am going home and will return in a week."

"Then please take your leave early if you like. We shall see you in one week. My dear, have you anything to say?" Stephen asked, looking at his contrite wife.

For the first time since they had entered the study, Annalise spoke. "Have a safe trip, Miss Bell, and return to us safely. Enjoy your stay and thank you for your patience today."

"I shall and don't worry, it was simply an off day."

"Yes."

Miss Bell left the room, and Stephen waved his wife to a sofa, walking behind her and sitting across from her.

"What have you to say about this afternoon's display of tempers, my dear?"

"Well, it is like Miss Bell said, milord. The day had turned, and things were unsettled."

"All right, then tell me what went wrong during your music lesson."

"What went wrong? Oh, well, I'm not quite sure. You know, when I get tired, my fingers won't work the way they should and then, well, after the fifth time trying to play the same notes, one becomes a bit annoyed, and by the tenth repetition without advancement, one becomes exasperated. Well, you know exasperation brings on discouragement, and that can frustrate and, well, ultimately anger one."

"I think I see. You had not practiced enough to complete the piece satisfactorily and, therefore, you threw a tantrum when you were unable to do as you were expected."

"I do so hate how you take my explanations of events and turn them into naughty revolts." Annalise jumped up.

"Sit down."

"But I want to... fine." Her reseating was less graceful the second time.

"I believe we understand that a tantrum is never allowed, not for Leesie and never for my Annalise. Go into my cabinet and take out my cane."

"Stephen, please, not the cane. It hurts so."

"When was the last time I used the cane on you?"

"Last week when I refused to ride the mount you chose for me."

"No, that was the crop. I believe I used the cane two weeks ago when you decided that a walk around the grounds would be a nice diversion and you went without a cloak and caught a great chill."

"Yes."

"Yes, the remnants of which are still evident. I don't believe making that choice has been a problem for you since."

"No, but why do I need music lessons?"

"You do because every woman of quality has music lessons at some point in their life. It helps with your entertainment, your solace when needed, numbers, confidence, and so many other things. So if you did not have lessons as a young child, then they are accomplished when you are older. We agreed it would help you with being Lady Thayer and fill your time. Now, go get the cane."

Without a word, she flounced past him and on to the cabinet behind him, making a great noise about retrieving it. She flung her arm out to him with the cane in her hand.

"You hold on to that. I find we need to have a little warm up first because you are in a rare temper that I find I do not like."

"You say you like my spark."

"Yes, but not your sizzle, so hold the cane and place yourself over my lap."

"Stephen, please?"

He chuckled. "That is too little, too late, my love. I think you have been spoiling for this all week. I mean to help you find a calmer inner self, so that you are happier."

"I'm happy. Indeed, I am. I just, oh, never mind," she said as she lay over her husband's knees.

The layers were more these days and while he understood it was for warmth, he missed the days of one petticoat and one chemise. Finding Annalise's bottom under the skirts was a chore he never tired of performing. He rubbed the pert globes and settled her so he had the best of her proffered derrière and he began his lesson on manners.

As he lectured on the way a lady should act, he landed two substantial slaps to her rear cheeks, which were met with a grunt of alarm. "I know you expected a few pats on the bottom, but I don't want to have this flagrant disregard for manners to continue. If you are angry, you excuse yourself until you have learned enough restraint to soldier on through the incident with decorum."

"But you would not have allowed me to leave just now."

"True, but if you could have communicated your increasing inability to be civil, I would have not taken such an offense, but as it is, you were rude to me, and that is not allowed. I daresay you were exceedingly rude to Miss Bell."

His hand landed another two sounds slaps and then two more before Annalise wiggled her discomfort. "I'm sorry, truly sorry."

"Not yet, but you will be. Right now you are sorry I did not put up with the behavior, soon you will be sorry that you demonstrated such behavior."

She sighed. "But I am out of sorts and not sure how to manage that appropriately. I don't know the cause, therefore I can't find the cure. But I am sorry, Stephen."

He peppered her seat with handprints, tipping her to reach the crease at her upper thighs, having finally found her sweet spot in both position and remorse.

"I'm sorry, Stephen, so very sorry. Honestly, I am. How do you handle your angst?"

"I would go for a walk, or go riding, neither of which are allowed you, unaccompanied. We shall come up with a plan. The better resolution is that you not get to that state."

He continued to spank, stopping to rub in between swats, and found his darling moaning and wiggling for another reason. Without another smack, the spanking was over, a lesson taught and hopefully learned. He rubbed the hurt out and felt his cock stand at attention. Her squeals turned to desperate moans, and he knew it was time to stop. There would be no gratification, as his wife liked to call it until the music incident was addressed.

Annalise issued a pouty sigh but did not complain when he sat her up and directed her and the cane to lead on to the music room, where he laid a stripe for every music sheet on the floor. There were six and after having her hold her skirts, he laid one line of fire after each sheet was picked up until all six were delivered.

"Since there are no lessons next week, you will spend an hour in the morning and an hour in the afternoon practicing this piece and any other music you are working on. Understood? I shall have you play for me at the end of the week."

"Yes, Stephen, but I am not good. I don't believe it is my aptitude."

"I daresay you will be much better after all those hours of practice. You will alert me to when you go in and alert me to your finishing. It will be a full hour each time, my girl, so do not try to spin me a tale."

"I won't."

"Excellent, now, shall we go for a ride?"

"Uh, no thank you, I believe I would not be able to sit my mount. Thank you."

"Ah, well, maybe a book on a nice soft cushion would do you better."

"A book?"

"Unless you would prefer a ride?"

"No, I am sure a book will be just the thing."

Stephen smiled out of sight of his wife while she found an appropriate book. He did so love her spirit.

Except for tutoring, soon the lessons of being Lady Thayer and Lady Annalise were over. It would just take practice now and time, both of which her husband provided plenty of. They had found a nice balance with Leesie as well.

They were in the sunroom enjoying their afternoon refreshment when Stephen reflected on their life. "I had envisioned Leesie being different but as my friend had pointed out to me while I despaired of finding a wife, that if I found the right woman, the rest would work itself out. And it certainly has. I am content how the playing of Leesie and Papa has turned out. It is just right for us."

Annalise sat down with Stephen and was cuddling into his lap as he was smoking his pipe and discussing the fruitfulness of his day. She loved these times because she could snuggle in, smell his good tobacco, and learn so much about the estate. She learned to understand how her husband thought on issues. She often tried to commit the information to memory so that she could recall it when needed. He already showed how impressed he was with her recall, as in French and recitations. She was continually trying to impress him even more with her lady's lessons, as she called the tutoring sessions. Almost as though she were earning her usefulness, which would have distressed Stephen for he saw her worth and tried to share his pride often.

Annalise was beginning to find the balance between yearning to feel that protection and that littleness with the natural unchallenged trust that being Leesie gave her, and the control of the rest of her world that Lady Thayer gave her. There was no question that when she was Anna with her husband, his undertaking of her training was more than successful. She was ready to give over to him and enjoy the physical satisfaction he offered her. Since he had taught her how he liked her to reciprocate, it had turned into even more enjoyable.

They had not had any guest save for Stephen's family on their random dropping in to say hello or discuss the estate, and the occasional vicar visit. A few times someone stopping by for quick delivery of a piece of information on their way through changed the dynamics of the day but little else. They had no overnight guests; they had no weekend shooting parties. She inquired about that with Stephen.

"Have you told all and sundry to stay away because you're ashamed of your wife or that she is incapable of representing you well?"

"What? Of course not." He was honestly confused. "Why would you say that? I would never say something like that to embarrass you or myself. However, I did keep people away for a while because I didn't want to overstress you or make you feel inadequate if you forgot one of the myriad rules associated with an over pompous society. I also wanted to have you all to myself for a while. We were also on our honeymoon, and I didn't want to be disturbed."

Annalise smiled. "Thank you. I quite understand that, and I appreciate it. But how am I to ever know if I am learning correctly if I don't have a chance to exercise those lessons?"

"Excellent observation. So, shall we have a small weekend party?"

"Define small."

"Ten or eleven, and we would make the twelfth couple. That is a good number."

"Twenty-four people?"

"Yes, my dear, twenty-four people are not considered excessive. That will fill our standard dining room table without an extra table, making it an excellent number. I have some men who I have enjoyed over the last years, and many are married. Of course, they do not need to be married. We will make up the numbers if there are un-shackled men who don't have a suggestion as to who should make up the numbers. Tell me when you're confident, and we will make it happen."

"Well, if it is to be that many, I might need a few more lessons with Mrs. Thorpe. But as soon as she says I am ready, I think we better try it."

"I await your instruction."

Chapter 17

Annalise was feeling much more satisfied with the way life had settled into a gratifying routine. She hadn't thought it possible on some days, but it had, mostly due to Stephen's efforts at not being the type of aristocrat that many others were. Meaning he cared about her, maybe even loved her and showed her often. He was generous, gentle, and kind. He encouraged through words and his thrashing hand for Annalise to do her best, and he rewarded her efforts often.

It was several weeks before the routine was disrupted again and this time it was due to the fact that Stephen had to go back into the city and Annalise did not want to go.

"Sweetheart, it will be for quite a long time, and I don't wish to leave you here alone." Stephen could not postpone his trip any longer. He had waited several weeks since the incident in the library, hoping for things to calm down. It had been a good decision, but now he needed to attend to business. As it was, January would be upon them by the time they returned.

"Why must I go with you? Traveling is cold. I can stay here, and you can go alone. I'll be fine," said Annalise while sitting at the breakfast table.

"Because I don't wish to leave you here, that is why. And you can't be avoiding the city for the rest of your life." Stephen showed his annoyance.

"What am I to do there? Nothing."

"There are plenty of things to do in the city while I am conducting business. Just the mere fact that you are my wife will open opportunities for you."

"Opportunities I have no desire to avail myself of."

"I'm not leaving you here, and that's the end of this conversation." Stephen continued his breakfast, speaking not another word.

"It is not settled. You can drag me along, of course, but I shall not be compliant. It will be very distasteful for you and there'll be no enjoyment for either of us."

"Annalise, you can be the most infuriating woman sometimes." Stephen got up, threw his napkin onto the table, and strode out of the room. His greatest display of anger had just shown itself. How could he be so calm all the time? Even in anger, he was subdued. It was unnatural.

Annalise had not had anything but an excellent rapport with Stephen since her night of disclosure several weeks before. And she wasn't sure why he was so adamant about her going with him. She had nothing to do with his business. She had no reason to be there, and yet he was still demanding. She had never seen him lose his temper with her. She knew that she would lose because her husband never took no for an answer if he expected yes to be the response.

Annalise was in the garden picking dead leaves off bushes and shuffling a path through the light snow on the ground, enduring the brisk crispness of the air when her husband came behind her and placed his hand gently on her shoulder.

"Are you all right?"

His voice sounded like a caress to her frayed and fragmented thoughts. She turned to her husband and smiled a tentative smile.

"Yes. I am. I am made of sturdier stuff."

"It is too cold to be out here long, my dear. Please come inside."

"I will in a few moments. I was thinking, and it clears my head to be outside rather than inside with the house around me. Here it's as though my thoughts have free rein without the proprieties and protocol that I feel indoors."

"I see. Why do you need your thoughts to have wings, my dear? Are you troubled?"

"Not really. I just don't know how to express my feelings about going back to the city, and I don't understand why it is so important to you that I go. I don't care if I ever return."

"Ah. I had thought as much. Here, walk with me into my study where the fire is warm, and we will figure this out, shall we?"

It took some conversation, but they were able to come to a compromise. If it were agreeable to both, it was decided that Annalise would go for a week and then return home to continue learning how to be Lady Thayer.

"I don't like letting you leave without me, traveling with only a maid and a footman for companionship but it will probably take several weeks and if I can get you to town, I am hoping you will stay for the duration."

"It is an agreeable compromise."

Stephen took Annalise's hand. "He cannot hurt you or even come to you."

"I know you are right, but," she shrugged. "The memories of being bartered..."

"Maybe your brother would be available for you. With escort, of course."

Annalise brightened. "I hadn't thought of that. I would stay for visiting for as long as he was able to visit. What an excellent idea, milord." She leaned over to kiss her husband. He held her tight and extended the kiss to more gratifying heights. "Now, about the hunt."

Annalise nodded. "I'm planning it to be grand. Mrs. Thorpe has been very helpful and I am following her lead to the letter. I believe I will be ready."

They had agreed earlier in the month to have a hunt near the end of the following month. The rather advanced planning was to take away all doubts about her performance. Annalise wanted to feel that her skills as Lady Thayer would not be less than perfect. It was not that Stephen cared one smidgen about whether his friends knew of her background, but he knew his wife wanted to make a good impression and feel she earned the pride he had in her.

He acquiesced with hesitation, but it was the only reason he would allow her to return early. It was a compromise they could both live with. He also knew when something was bothering her that she had yet to work out, so he hoped this time and the change of scenery would allow that issue to work it out. He did wonder how long it would take his mother to make an appearance. So far, she had held out and stayed away. Luckily, no one else did, and Annalise felt the full support of the other family members.

Stephen took Annalise to something every evening while she was in London and did not entice her to go where she did not wish to go. He knew that they would need to travel to London several times a year, and he needed her to get rid of the rancid taste of the city she endured and replace it with the sweetness of how it could be now.

It seemed as though she was not well upon rising of a morning, but it was soon past, and she was not afflicted the rest of the day. Maybe it was her nerves, but nonetheless, Annalise went to musical recitals and a dinner party that included no less than fifty people. The experience was good, but she was thankful her husband settled for twenty-four as their guest number.

The theater was incredible, and Stephen was the consummate escort. Stephen's efforts to make her stepfather see reason to allow Jules to visit his sister never produced any satisfaction. So, after two weeks in London, Annalise had sampled enough for one trip and her husband, more than pleased with her participation, bundled her up and promised to see her in a few weeks' time.

"You are not to pleasure yourself, my dear, while I am gone." Her look of confusion prompted him to be more clear. "You cunny. You may not touch it until I am home and I will give you pleasure."

"That isn't nice, Stephen. Not when you have been so attentive to my... needs,"

"I have and I plan to be that attentive again, but you will have to wait until I have arrived home. Promise me."

"Must I?"

His smile was full of carnal knowledge. "Oh, yes. Pledge to me."

"Yes, fine. I give you my promise." She pouted, and he kissed her lips. It would be a long few weeks.

Stephen was to be gone for another fortnight, and during his absence, Annalise worked hard to understand those things she needed to know. The London experience helped her tremendously to see people in action, enjoying things she had only dreamed of. It was actually freeing to have Stephen gone so she could meet her own schedule. She woke early in the day, ate and went back to sleep until later. Then she was up and she created her own schedule that included a pretend dinner party that the staff helped her through. She was ecstatic with the results, but she missed her husband.

Finally, when it was almost time for Stephen to return and begin preparing for the shooting party, she spent a whole day in role-play as Lady Thayer. Annalise embarked on the enactments with alacrity. She practiced all manner of situations that could occur during entertaining and being entertained. That the staff assisted in enthusiastically took Anna's nervousness away.

As Lady Thayer, she served tea and made polite but interesting conversation having been schooled by Mr. Thorpe on the current events of the day. He agreed to provide interesting tidbits daily and took his duty seriously. He also instructed her ladyship on how to receive and send off her guests as well as how to be received and depart herself.

Mrs. Thorpe had spent weeks with Annalise, working on how to run the household. It was exhausting work but gratifying as things became more natural to Annalise. Mrs. Thorpe showed and practiced daily Annalise's responsibilities and what were the housekeeper's responsibilities.

Mrs. Roundtree helped with appropriate menus and the timing of meals as well as acceptable offerings for different occasions. Mr. Roundtree, who was the head groundskeeper for the Hall, offered to show her a book of botanicals in the library and discreetly marked the ones in their gardens. He said it wasn't fair to expect her to know them as she had never seen them in bloom as of yet. Lady Thayer gratefully accepted and kept the book within easy reach.

Once they had done all they could, Annalise endured the pianoforte lessons her husband had insisted upon. Her voice was untrained but quite lovely, and Miss Bell stated how impressed she was with not only her musical talents but also her stitchery. While not expected to be any shining star in any of the areas, Annalise was, by now, quite passably good and had a wonderful scene in progress on her embroidery stand. Once that was complete, she was to go on to needlepoint and wool knitting.

"I am much better at wool-gathering, I am afraid," stated Lady Thayer to her teacher. That reasonably young but overly focused woman, kind though she was, did not see the humor. In fact, her ladyship feared she had confused the woman.

Overall, the intense work was paying off, and when Annalise missed a step, someone was there to cue her to the right one. Her confidence soared, and she was anxious to see her husband. For while she had worked hard, she sorely missed him. Lady Thayer wanted to show off her newly acquired skills and talents. Anna wanted to sleep next to her warm husband in his bed and Leesie was becoming overwhelmed and need some papa time. And while he was gone, she slept in her own bed. It was dreary, cold and becoming disheartening in her room, but she couldn't bear to sleep in his bed without him.

Two days later, Annalise was awakened in the dark of night by her bed moving. She screamed in the haze of her brain and tried to push the intruder out of her bed when she heard a familiar voice.

"Annalise, listen. It is me, Stephen."

Hearing his voice as well as his hand over her mouth stopped her screams, but not her anger at being frightened so ruthlessly.

"Get out. Get out of my bed, you scoundrel."

"What? I have told you it is your husband, not some stray cull set to do you harm."

"My husband would have been mindful of his wife's sensibilities and not given her such a fright," Annalise declared, still not calmed from her scare.

Stephen's voice was contrite and demanding. "I apologize that I teased you, but I will not leave this bed tonight. Mine is cold and empty, and I have spent too many nights in it alone. I intend to sleep in my house only with my wife. Haven't you missed me?"

She relented, for she had missed him terribly. "Yes, I have missed you so much I hurt for want of you."

"Then let me take the hurt away."

His hands roamed her body and divested her of the night gown without much hesitation. His clothing came off with equal ease. The kissing and touching started sweet and loving but soon became desperate and passionate. He caressed and tweaked her nipples. She squealed her sensitivities.

"Have you hurt your breasts?" asked Stephen, who missed nothing when it came to his wife.

"I am more tender, milord, but I am not sure why."

"Hmm, then let us treat them with kindness until they feel less sore."

His mouth landed on her belly and worked its way down to her lady bits. "Open yourself to me, Anna. I have a great hunger for your treats."

Her moan accompanied her wanton display of her pinkness and jumped when Stephen flicked her clit. "Have you been naughty?"

"No, but I have cursed you plenty these last weeks. It was a cruel thing to ask of me."

His chuckle was full of devilish delight. "Good girl. I am happy you complied, so I must now reward my darling with sparkles and fireworks."

The fireworks were indeed a grand show. One that was reenacted many times that night and into the morning for both lord and lady. When Annalise finally opened her eyes, the next day, it was nearly midday. She ate the toast that had begun to arrive at her bedside for over a week now, and she was glad for it. Whoever thoughtfully had left it must have noticed her habit of the morning and thought to help. She was grateful today.

The preparations for the hunting party were in the final stages of completion. As the activity in the manor began to grow with everyone's focus on the upcoming event, Annalise started to feel her fears rising. The staff had continued to throw scenarios and instances her way, trying to catch her in practice so it would not happen in reality. She continued to do quite well and her confidence to perform as Lady Thayer, with the staff at least, was complete.

"I believe everything is ready for your friends to come to the hunting party." Annalise started the conversation once her husband had settled into his seat at breakfast one morning after he had returned. "I'm feeling the anxiety of not showing you well, Stephen. I'm having difficulty focusing and it's annoying. And it's also annoying because I have nothing else with which to focus my attention."

Stephen could see her agitation in her rearranging of the silver-ware and the teasing of the food on her plate. Placing his napkin on his lap, he leaned closer to his wife.

"You are rather anxious. I have just a little work this morning that needs to be addressed, and then I'm all yours. What should you like to do today?"

"Well, I can assure you we can do nothing outside. Have you seen the weather? I believe it's gotten worse rather than better as the time approaches."

"It is yet the end of December, my dear. Spring and better weather is a few months away. While we are marching on towards calmer weather, it is a distance away. And look, I believe you are engaged in small talk. Had you noticed?" She shook her head. "You have nothing to worry about."

"So what shall we do if picnicking on the lawn is out?" he teased his wife, but she was too preoccupied to notice.

"Well, I believe I have been quite attentive to the occasion that possibly I could have some relief from the planning responsibility. Just for a few hours, you understand." Annalise did not look at her husband but was quite sure he would understand her request.

"Ah, so this relief from responsibility as Lady Thayer would give you the relief you feel you need and have earned. Am I correct?"

Stephen had no compunction about watching for his wife's spo-ken and unspoken responses. She had flattened the table napkin and replaced it in her lap. She drew up her hands from straightening her dress, and she was now back to teasing her food. He reached over and placed his hand on hers to still them in their task of torment.

"Is it that we need to find if there is a papa in the house?" He said it as a simple question and began eating his sausages as he waited for his Leesie to respond.

Annalise let out a quiet but audible breath of relief. She was not going to have to ask any more directly than she had. Stephen had picked up on her need immediately. This was the first time that she had asked. All other times Stephen had announced it for one reason or another or she had fallen into it unwittingly. Today, she needed the diversion and was happy that she was able to ask.

"That would be wonderful. And I could go find Leesie. I'm sure she must be in the house somewhere."

"Yes, I daresay she is."

"In fact, it is very possible that she might come to this very breakfast table this morning."

"Really? Brilliant, for I am equally sure that her papa could come to the breakfast table this morning."

"Yes? Now?"

"Now."

Chapter 18

With the next words out of Annalise's mouth, she became Leesie and the stressors of the responsibilities that she must carry during most days began to slide off, allowing her to pull on the much lighter mantle of being young and precocious. The responsibilities of the day did not belong to her, they belonged to her papa.

"Oh, I need to go change my clothing. This isn't appropriate at all." Leesie began to stand up quickly, but her papa reached over and grabbed her hand, stopping all upward movement.

"Sit down, my sprite. You're perfectly fine until you've finished your breakfast."

Leesie's Papa was indeed in the room, and his voice brooked no argument. It thrilled her and gave her tingles all through her body, but she pouted anyway.

"Look at me. This just won't do."

Her eyes were wide and her complaint obvious. The long days with proper adult day dress that Annalise liked very much, and the attire that Lady Thayer showed off, Leesie could not bear to wear. In fact, her over dramatization began to rise quite quickly at the thought that she might have to wear the dress she had on rather than one of her short frocks with plenty of frilly, fluffy petticoats. She would have to stay in their rooms when wearing them, but she was quite content to do so.

"Please, papa?"

They had connecting doors connecting her rooms with his and a joined sitting room. The rooms encompassed a whole wing. She had even found the back stairway to a darkened corridor to sneak into her papa's study, the library, and even the family sitting room if she wanted to. She had often left her rooms, slipped into the sitting room with its hidden sweetmeats, and returned before ever being discovered.

Her papa looked over at her sanguinely. "Yes, I understand. But we are at the table now, and so you will finish breakfast first before you go to change. I'll not have us coming off schedule because you didn't think ahead." Stephen calmly began to eat his breakfast again.

"That is unfair, Papa. I had no idea of the requirements of my day. I had thought they would be as they were yesterday, and, therefore, I dressed appropriately. And now that my plans have changed, so must I."

She waited expectantly for him to agree so that she could run and pick out the frocks she wanted. She knew exactly the one she was going to wear. It was the china blue one that was very close to her eye color. And she was good at brushing her long hair out after dislodging her pins. She could think of all the things that she needed to do and wanted to do, and yet here she was required to sit at the table to eat food she could cheerfully do without. She'd already eaten her bread, after all.

"Papa does not wish to start off the day setting his young lady straight. But if she needs it, when I am done with my breakfast, I will accommodate adjusting her behavior, or if she pushes it, before then."

He looked straight at Leesie and waited for her to answer. He did not have to wait long, for the frustrated moan that came out of her mouth made him want to smile. He restrained himself, knowing it was not what she needed right now. She needed him to be firm, and being firm was something of which he was quite adept.

"You simply don't understand the requirements of young ladies, Papa."

"Yes, well, I certainly do know the requirements of this papa for his young lady, and that is all I need to know. Shall I cut your meat?"

"Yes, please."

Breakfast finished, Leesie skipped up the stairs to change her clothing while her papa completed his morning business. He instructed her to play with her dolls, and he would come back and retrieve her when he concluded his business. In the beginning, she was quite happy to do that, but in her inpatient mind, when she had dressed and played for a short period of time, she expected him to come get her. He had yet to do that and in her little girl thinking she was impatient, scrambling to find a way to circumvent the restriction. Knowing that she was not to leave her bedroom or her playroom, Leesie tried her best to entertain herself. But as was hard for most children, Leesie was unable to maintain her interest for long.

Finally, unable to occupy herself any longer, she began looking for her papa. It was unfortunate that she chose that moment to leave, for had she waited not five minutes more, she would have been greeting her papa as he strode into her bedroom. However, that was not to be the case, and she trotted down the stairs. She knew it was the busy time of the day for the staff and, therefore, was not worried about discovery.

Unfortunately, she rounded the corner just as a gentleman was exiting her papa's study with her papa. While she had seen them just in time and the visitor only caught a snatch of cloth going around the corner, her papa did not miss a thing. He bid his guest goodbye and went in search of his errant sprite.

Leesie went through one of the connecting doors under the staircase, entering the stairwell and quietly closed the door behind her. She then walked very carefully along the wall because she did not have a candle to light her path. For a moment, fear burned in her chest, for she thought she had lost her way, but then she saw a glimmer of light under a doorway. That helped her reorient herself. That doorway was her papa's study. She dared not open that door.

As she crept by the study, hoping to open the door to the gallery a distance down the passageway, she tripped, bumping the study panel. The door opened suddenly, and she found her arm grabbed and she was pulled unceremoniously into her papa's study.

"And what do we have here, a robber seeking gold or a little sprite not doing as she was told?" It was obvious to both the speaker and the listener the answer to the riddle.

"That rhymes Papa," she said brightly.

"Leesie."

"Well, you were taking ever so long. A lady cannot wait forever, you know. It is deemed to be very rude to keep a lady waiting." Her words were full of bravado, but as she snuck a look up at her papa, it began to seep away quickly.

"Be that as it may, you know the rules. If Papa says to do something, you must always do it. To not mind his words is to court a hot bottom. Is that what you need, Leesie, a hot bottom? For I can assure you, no lady would enter from the panel door, regardless of how long she is kept waiting."

It was evident that her papa was not going to accept anything but a response. And unconsciously Leesie knew that while she may not want to want it, she desperately needed a spanking to relieve her stress. The pressure of preparing for the dreaded eventuality of performing her task as Lady Thayer to the world was indeed oppressive at times. She knew she needed the release and that only as Leesie did she have the permission to release all responsibility.

She hung her head in nonverbal defeat, however Papa was not going to accept that as a response from her. He lifted her chin up and while he was firm, there was a little sparkle in his eye and gentleness in his word when he spoke.

"I need you to answer me, my little sprite. Papa has seen you spend hours working on a project, so I know that lack of ability to attend to something is not a problem. But I do think you just need your papa to take control. I think that's why you lost patience so quickly. You knew that if you did not do as you were told, there would be retribution. So maybe your papa takes control today, so we put the world right again. Eh?"

She nodded her head in the small space he gave her while still retaining her chin and she tried to drop her eyes, but it was too difficult. He was holding her up at an angle that didn't quite lend itself to total obscurity.

"Yes, Papa."

And that's all it took for Stephen to change roles and to take over doing as papas do with errant little girls. He walked her very gently but purposely to the sofa in his study and sat down in the middle of it. She knew her place, and it was to his right, and when he patted his left knee, she folded her body over his thighs. It wasn't difficult to toss up her petticoats. They pretty much tossed up themselves. He simply pushed them out of the way, and when he saw that she had undergarments, he removed them.

"Do not put these back on today. In fact, Leesie should always ask permission to wear undergarments. It dispenses with the removal when Papa must warm her little bottom."

"But it is unseemly to show one's bottom to the world, Papa. And Leesie is not always naughty."

"And so it is, so if I forbid the undergarments, it means you are to stay in your rooms." His voice softened. "And no, my Leesie is not often naughty, but she is in need of submission often."

He rubbed her back to relax her, as he could hear her breathing change to a familiar cadence. The shallow, fast breath of her submission to him. He then began to attend to her upturned cheeks. His hand landed easier at first, just to coax the blood to the surface because he never wanted to bruise his little sprite.

"Stop wiggling, sprite. I don't want to strike the wrong spot."

"Papa, can we be done now?"

His chuckle wasn't entirely contained. "You have little patience for anything today, sweetling. We will be done when I am done. Hush."

He rubbed and spanked with ever-increasing strokes until he was well and truly heating a fire where his hand connected with her ever-pinkening flesh.

"Papa, I'm sorry. Papa, please stop."

But the request was halfhearted, and Stephen knew his wife by now. She needed more. She needed much more. In fact, she would be disappointed and unfulfilled if he didn't complete the task to meet her needs and even a step further. He intended to be that person for her because she was that person for him. She fulfilled his needs and more and he would do no less for her.

He stood her up and bade her stand still as he walked over to his desk drawer and opened it. Reaching inside, he pulled out a small, thin baton that he had brought back from London on this last trip. He kept it in his study drawer for just such an occasion as this. He watched Leesie's eyes grow round as the processes of her brain filled in her questions.

"No, Papa. I promise to be good. Papa, please just use your hand."

He could hear a little more urgency, but still quite unconvincing. No, he was doing the right thing. As he sat back in the middle of the sofa, he was a little surprised at how quickly and easily his little one slid over his knee. While not quite anxious to resume her spot, not reticent either. If nothing else, she was curious.

"Do you wonder about the sting this little baton will have on your bottom?"

"A little, Papa, but also, a little fearful."

"I'll be very careful, but I think you need more."

He swatted her a few more times to reheat the burn he had left the moments before he had gotten up. Then he reached for the rather thin reed baton that he had laid across the small of her back, and he felt her tense. He soothed her with one hand rubbing her back and encouraging her with his words and as soon as he felt her relax he laid a stripe across her lower fleshy bottom. Her accompanying screech told him he had done it right.

Line after angry line, he slowly methodically touched the implement to her backside, tipping her to pay particular attention to the sensitive, sweet spot between the north and south of his previously attended areas. He concluded his efforts at releasing her tensions by laying several more stripes across the top of her thighs. While she had not begun to actually cry, he could feel her body relax.

Putting the instrument down, he spoke. "Leesie, Papa is going to use his hand again to finish this off. It is imperative that you stop thinking about everything else. Think about Papa and his hand slapping your bottom with no escape. Release yourself to me. Release your anger and your frustrations to me. Give your anxiety to Papa because it's his job to handle all of that. It's not Leesie's job."

With no other fanfare and waiting for no response from her, he spanked. He spanked rhythmically but quickly up and down one thigh over the cheek and down the other side, ending at the second thigh. It was then that it happened. He spread her to give him the room to slap her inner thighs. That mournful cry and cleansing relief that was particular to his wife when she let go of the burdens that were becoming too heavy for her. He was waiting for the sound of that response, the signal that she was where she needed to be and he should take her just a step further.

"You are not to be a mischievous sprite. Do you feel my hand? It is to remind you that I am the grown-up, the one who must control things, not you. You are to do as you are told."

He increased the strength of his slaps just enough to leave that sizzling burn that she would carry with her the rest of the day. He grinned because Leesie never went into the night except for that one incident several months ago. However, Lady Thayer had been required to deal with a sensitive backside on more than a few occasions, and Annalise lamented the time it took to lose sensitivity while her husband pounded out his need between her thighs.

He knew this would ignite other things in his little sprite that they did not address while she was Leesie. He was very careful about the distinction because it was vital to him and he felt to her as well that Leesie stayed a little girl. Anna was his wife in bed. He knew that their evening would be just as exciting as the day today.

Two more times he tossed his lovely young lady over his knee in the course of the day neither one near the intensity of the morning spanking but just enough to reheat and reaffirm his love for her. The last time was when they were having late afternoon tea to tide them over for a nice adult dinner later in the evening.

"Papa, I don't like this."

Leesie indicated a type of sandwich that included the grinding of liver and tongue. Her grimace and the pushing the way of her food, she knew, was unacceptable behavior. Instead, her hand reached over to grab a morsel of cake, only to have the extended hand slapped soundly. In her indignant response, she looked up at him ready to do battle, only it was obvious that the battle had already been lost. Stephen stood and quickly lifted her up and leaned her over the arm of the sofa. One more quick movement removed the obstacle of her skirts, and he peppered her bottom rapidly and diligently. A dozen slaps landing in an order she was unable to figure out before the punishment was over.

For this round, she kicked, screamed and yelled because she was totally free and purged after her day. She was now simply the six-year-old getting her bottom spanked for her impertinence. Tears came quickly and were turned off just as quickly when the spanking concluded. When she sat down, she grimaced at the pressure on her well-chastised bottom and her potted meat sandwich still sitting in front of her. She tried a different tactic to see if it would work.

In her sweetest voice, she asked, "Papa, I don't care for this sandwich filling. Might I trade for a different type?" She looked up at him with hopeful eyes that he could not ignore.

"Yes, you may. But do understand that won't always be an option to you."

"Yes, Papa. Thank you." Leesie finished her tea calmly, ready to make her transition. She went to lie down for a short rest before changing her clothes. Serenity restored.

Chapter 19

The day of the first arrivals presented crisp and clear and all at Thayer Hall hoped the weather would hold for the entire week. However, all understood that in the month of January, any weather could present and they had every contingency covered. Their guest would not find themselves languishing for lack of appropriate entertainment available to them.

James and his wife were among those participating in the festivities during the day, as was Stephen's father, however, his mother did not acknowledge the invitation. A fact that Stephen had to explain quite plaintively to his distraught wife.

"Sweetheart, mother is not going to ignore us forever. We will have children and she will want to be a part of their lives. To do that, she will have to not only build a relationship with you, but she will also have to apologize for her terrible treatment of you."

"I just want her to accept me as your wife. I know I'm not as good as the others, and I don't matter the same. I wish she knew how much I love you and I worry it will hurt your relationship with her."

"I love you so much, my darling. Do not worry about mother. It will happen, sweetling. It will happen."

Lady Thayer, while nervous, was in full form. She walked around the Hall as lady of the house and indeed she felt as though everything within these walls and all on the grounds possessed by her husband did indeed also belong to her. She was beginning to come into her own, and this would be the final introduction to her husband's society. She would be established after this week. Stephen had been careful in his selection of participants to ensure that.

Stephen didn't worry what his friends thought, for he had no doubts that his beautiful wife could meet her obligations without mishap, for he thought her perfect for him. Annalise wished that she had the same nonchalant attitude about the whole affair. However, she feared that would never happen. She sufficed with the confidence that she felt through practice in her role and continued.

By midday, the first guest had arrived. Other than Annalise trying to open the door instead of letting Mr. Thorpe to his duties, to which he presented her a stern look, her receiving of their first guests went without a hitch. The guests were now up in their bedchambers, and with assistance, settling in. So went the rest of the first day.

Dinner was sparkling and vividly enchanting as Lady Thayer took in all that was transpiring in her seemingly fairytale world. She sat back quietly for a moment, while others laughed, ate and consumed an enormous amount of wine in wonderment. This was truly her home, and these were her guests. She turned to look towards her husband and marveled that he was indeed her husband. She admired the way that he conversed with ease and transitioned to another conversation and another activity without missing a beat. She wondered if it were ever to be that simple for her.

The men went shooting the second day while the women found a variety of activities at their disposal inside. The weather was quite chilly, and the indoor sports were more to their liking. In the sitting room, there was needlework set out, and in the music room, sheet music was available, as were the piano, harp, and violin. The flute was offered, but none picked it up. Card tables were set up, but Stephen had made the announcement at dinner the first night that no woman was allowed to bet with money in his home.

"It is a rather vile habit for men at times and is always a vulgarity for women. We have prepared colored wood sticks to simulate the gamble, if you desire." There were several disappointed guests, but as she didn't even know how to gamble, Annalise felt no loss.

Annalise enjoyed the conservatory and found a kindred soul in a young woman named Lady Charlotte. The woman was not married long herself and Annalise enjoyed the comradery offered her.

"Are you sure you are not from the area I was raised for there was an Annalise Coton that I played with as a very young child."

"I left my original home ten years ago."

"Yes, that would be about right. My friend also left. Wait, I was called Lottie then."

"Oh, you're Lottie? Forgive me, I haven't thought of you for years. I am so happy to reacquaint myself with you. Tell me again where it is, for I cannot even recall."

"Grimsby, in Lincolnshire, north of here, is where you come from. Why did you leave?"

Annalise spent the rest of the evening catching up and filling in all the gaps that were left when she was forced from her family home. According the Charlotte, who had just visited her family very recently, Annalise's uncle had died from some sickness. His son, however, was in possession of the home now, but he didn't want it.

"So it is to sit abandoned?"

"It has these last two years. I believe he is going to sell it in the spring. If you want any of the things, you must see if your husband will take you and allow you some purchases."

"It was encumbered, so how could he sell it?"

Charlotte shrugged. "If you own it, you can sell it, I imagine. Ask your Lord Thayer to explain it."

They decided to have Stephen send an inquiry straightaway. Charlotte gave her directions and invited them to stay with her and her husband while inquiring.

"We are not there all the time as my in-laws are near here and we come when we can."

Several women joined the conversation, and the talk turned to more universal interests.

When the men came down for dinner after changing and cleaning up from the shooting excursion, Charlotte and Annalise waylaid them and excitedly filled them in on the information uncovered.

Lord Richard Raine, the third Earl of Teague, reiterated the invitation his wife had issued and plans were made to go in a fortnight.

That evening, as they were preparing for bed, Annalise snuggled into the arms of her husband and sighed in contentment.

"What are you so satisfied with, my dear?"

"I cannot believe that I have met a childhood friend that remembered me and still lives in the shire I used to live with my parents. I had thought that part of my life was gone forever. I cannot tell you how it makes me yearn to see the country there again."

"And I cannot tell you how seeing you happy makes me happy. I feel I must caution you that there is likely to be some disappointment in attempting to relive childhood memories that may not have survived to today."

"Oh, I know, but I must try to capture what I can, mustn't I?"

"Yes, without a doubt. We shall enjoy the trip."

"Yes," she answered as she drifted off to enjoy a peaceful slumber.

The next day, Annalise walked up to a group of women who had their backs to her. Just as she was about to open her mouth, she heard her name come out of one of theirs. It was possibly the elegant woman named Lady Constance who spoke. When the woman spoke again, Annalise was quite confident it was that woman.

"You know, of course, he picked her up off some street and brought her home. We all thought she must've been with child, but it was a ruse to get him to marry her, because he is honorable. He would have made all the appropriate arrangements. Or—"

"Or," chimed in the second of three women whom she thought one held the name of Lady Isabella, "he was in his cups, which I think is the more believable story, for what peer marries because of a mishap? In any case, poor Stephen, for he's saddled with her for the rest of his life. It's a good thing he has such excellent standings, for while we won't accept her into our circles, we would never exclude him. We still have a place of solace for him when he's done with whatever it is she provides him."

"I have a delicious piece of information that I was told I should not disclose, but I'm positive that you two will be the height of discretion."

Lady Jane, the most pompous of all, thought she had some juicy information about Annalise, and try as she might, she could not interrupt them. She had an unnatural fascination in hearing the uncharitable words being spoken about herself. Annalise did not move while the women, still believing themselves to be alone, promised their voices to be silenced and their lips to be sealed. If she weren't trying so hard to stay silent herself, Annalise would have barked out her laughter of disbelief.

"Well, a woman in my mother's employ, her companion, was hired to do a task for Lady Chantelle Moulton. She came here as a nanny or something. I have it on great authority that Mrs. Mason has said that Lady Thayer sometimes takes on the act of a child."

Annalise almost swooned, something she'd never done in a situation such as this before. She had been embarrassed many times, disrespected, had to fight off unwanted advances, and even learned words that would put the saltiest of characters to blush. But what this woman was saying bit to the core of Annalise and her marriage. Gossip like that would be a scandal that destroyed reputations. Hers didn't mean anything but Stephen's was impeccable. It would not do for it to be tarnished.

The ability to be who she needed to be when she needed to be it was private. And the fact that anyone knew of the manifestation of that need of either her or Stephen surpassed mortification. Before thinking, she let out a pained yelp.

All three women shrieked and turned to stare into the face of the woman they just maligned. Their hostess. All three faces turned quite white and then bright red at the chagrin of having been caught tongue wagging. Annalise was about to say something when she saw Lady Jane's husband, Lord Thomas Whittenbrach, began to approach and she knew either she said it now, or she said it not at all. Unfortunately, the hurt inside her refused to stay unspoken.

Tossing all caution to the wind, Annalise spoke clearly to the woman. "And how is it that this companion of your mother's would have any knowledge of the inner workings of my life or my home?" Her tone was deceivingly even and yet blazingly angry.

Either the woman was addle-brained, which Annalise was quite positive could have been the case, or she was throwing caution to the wind as she responded in a haughty tone.

"That woman was employed in your home for a week and said she was part of the process of you becoming a small child and acting the same."

Annalise answered quick as a whip, "And if she is your mother's companion and if your statement were true, that would be quite a dark disclosure about your own mother's life choices. Interesting. It is so interesting, in fact, that I might find it a challenge to keep that information quiet. Coming from the woman's own daughter, no one would doubt the veracity of it, surely."

Just as Annalise was saying her final piece, Lord Thomas had come upon them and his hearing, unfortunately being quite sharp, heard her last response.

"Lady Annalise," that fine gentleman began, "I feel compelled to discuss with your husband the merits of your statement."

"I daresay that you feel quite compelled, but I encourage you to think about it. For should you find the need to discuss this conversation with my husband, I shall also be equally obliged to disclose your wife's indiscretions to which I was answering. I don't mind recounting them to you at this moment if you like," she offered.

That gentleman, apparently having known some of his wife's tendencies, gave the same a stern look. That ill-spoken woman, evidently having experienced her husband's displeasure before, had the good grace to step in.

"Honestly, Thomas, truly, it was a misunderstanding. I am positive that I mistook a conversation earlier in the week and, upon discussion with Lady Thayer, find I am reticent to pursue the unsubstantiated statements."

Thomas took his exit quite quickly as if he were thankful to be allowed to flee unscathed. He was the only one left authorized to do that. Annalise turned to the three women before allowing herself to give them a dark look.

She told them in barely controlled contempt, "And you three, should you find the need to spread poisonous gossip while in attendance at my home again, I shall turn the lot of you out without a care of the time or circumstance." She turned on her heel and walked away stiffly, elegantly, and seething in anger.

THAT EVENING IN THEIR bedchamber, Stephen, who had been the consummate host, explained his displeasure to his wife.

"Annalise, what were you about today with Lord Thomas and his wife, Lady Jane? You're the hostess and are not allowed to berate the guests."

Annalise twirled around, half undressed, obviously uncaring at the sight it presented. Stephen had to school his mind to focus on the issue at hand and not that he wanted his hands on his gorgeous wife. His cock was begging for attention.

"How dare you! You have no idea what I have put up with these last few days. You have gone off on the hunt, or the shoot or whatever you care to call this gathering and have entertained yourself on horseback with the dogs and with men who find gossip of the deeply personal kind distasteful."

"While I wish that were the case, it isn't always." Some of his anger left at what he considered a joke of sorts.

"It is not amusing."

Annalise began gesturing and walking along the circuit of the room in her undress. It was easy to see that she was very affected by some situation of which he was not privy. Stephen had learned to interpret this behavior quite accurately. He knew there must be something else going on. He lowered his tone just slightly to give it a slight rumble.

"Then enlighten me as to what it is." His voice had gone very quiet, very calm. It was the voice that unnerved Annalise more than any other tone that he used. He had found that when things seemed as though getting to the crux of the matter was going to be trying, this voice created a much quicker, more agreeable outcome.

"What it is, Stephen, is a house full of pompous asses. They have no thought of another person save themselves, and no thought of what might be proper. They think that because I was not born into an aristocracy, which we now know isn't even accurate, that I cannot possibly know what people should do in polite society. You don't have to be born into anything other than the human race to find out what is considered common courtesy and simple kindness."

"Yes, I have known a few of these women to open their mouths often finding shoe leather shoved inside, but tell me of the incident today. For I can tell you, the part of it that I had retold to me was not flattering to you, my dear."

"Of course, it was unflattering to me. My Lord, do you not understand that it will forever be the case? People will always look down on your wife, people will always say rude and nasty things about her either to her face, and if they're extremely bold, to yours as well. They will always have the opinion in agreement with your mother. I am not and never will be good enough for you."

"I dare the man or woman to try to discredit my wife or to say anything untoward about her within my hearing or to my knowledge."

Annalise's shoulders drooped, and her hand came up in a telltale nervous gesture to touch her hair and then she began pulling out the pins holding it up in an elegant style that she didn't feel was proper for her to wear. She wasn't elegant, no matter how much she tried to pretend. She wasn't this woman of the ton or a diamond in the rough she was just the daughter of a lord who didn't live long enough to make better provisions for his wife and daughter. A man turned Navy sailor in honor of his country because he didn't think of his family. She was merely a girl whose mother had passed away, leaving her to a merchantman who thought nothing more than to use her and then sell her. Why should she expect more from anyone else?

Stephen reached over and slid the palm of his hand down her hair, running his hands under its curtain to the nape of her neck, grasping it and pulling her towards his demanding lips. He kissed her hard, almost violently, and she answered in kind. She needed this type of release: hard, angry, punishing, and honest.

Stephen lifted up and took a step back, but not releasing her and in a voice ragged with emotion, he said, "What happened? How did they hurt you?"

Chapter 20

She leaned into his chest and took a deep breath, inhaling the scent that was her husband. She tried to swallow a sob that was unsuccessful. He drew her close and covered her with a woolen throw on the high-backed chair near the bed. Then he held her close while she gained her composure, as she knew he worked hard to do himself. If she were hurt, her husband wanted to stop the pain. Good Lord how she loved him.

Finally, she looked up with tears in her blue eyes and said, "It doesn't matter. None of it matters but you. Please don't be angry with me. I defended my honor, but I didn't need to. There isn't anything to defend."

Annalise looked at the confusion on Stephen's face. She could tell he wasn't quite sure how to take this information. She saw him appear to accept what she said out of hand, as something she needed to say, not that he needed to totally understand.

"Are you saying you have no honor to defend? That talk will earn you a serious thrashing if it is. You must tell me. I'm not angry, more perplexed. If I promise not to respond, will you tell me?"

"Suffice to say that the woman who claimed you had spoken for her hand has spoken against me. Our private lives, thanks to her and a Mrs. Mason, now the personal assistant to the mother of Lady Jane. Evidently, Mrs. Mason, as the story goes, stayed here a week and she assisted in the process of me becoming and acting like a small child. It appears that woman was paid to do this by Lady Chantelle Moulton."

"I see. I apologize for not telling you that I did know a small portion of it before now." He grabbed her hand and sat with her pulled on his lap.

"I received a response to the letter of inquiry I sent to Lord Gaston as to the reference Mrs. Mason produced. He did not write it, as I suspected, but who the woman was, how she answered an ad that was only placed in a private, very exclusive men's club, I have no idea." He seemed to relax and leaned down to give her another kiss. "And I will have a conversation with Thomas and settle the matter very quietly, but completely."

"No, I mean, please do not make this worse than it is. I will have to live with things being as they are and hope you are not maligned too much on my behalf."

"Do not worry. Now that I know who it is who has caused all the trouble, this particular problem will go away. If there comes more gossip of a different type later, I shall deal with it then. Tonight, your only concern is to love your husband."

"I do love you, my lord. That is a fact to be shared."

"Ah, tonight, you may refer to me as my lord, for I intend to be your lord and master."

His dominance allowed her to release all of her emotion into what her husband could give her. He could give her physical release and feed that part of her so completely.

"Just take me; please don't talk about anything else to do with anyone else but being here loving each other."

She tried to communicate, in the way that she spoke, the desperate need that she had for her husband and his special brand of loving. He must've understood her, for he bound her tight, giving her the freedom to rail and fight against those bindings and then fall into their release. He took her hard and fast, treating her body almost cruelly, and yet she used her body to tease him, taunting his responses. He delighted in reaching for those responses and reveling in the pleasurable pain that they brought her. Purging her emotional ache and mental anguish in an almost savage way, obliterating all of those hurts, thoughts, and feelings that she couldn't purge any other way.

Sweating and heaving from her exertion for the last time this evening, she closed her eyes in complete exhaustion, with no more muscle strength left. She lay in the middle of the bed, watching her husband untie her bindings. He ran his hands over her body lovingly, gently taking inventory to verify her skin remained unblemished and kissing any areas ravaged too violently.

"You should not have allowed me such free and passionate reign over your body tonight. I wanted you more than I could control, my dear. It was unconscionable of me.."

"I love when you are rough. Not all the time, but tonight was what I needed to release all my stress and anger."

"We may add this to one of the methods to take your mind off the responsibilities of the day."

He kissed her inner thigh before placing Anna's body just so on his bed and climbed in behind her, drawing her against his skin and spooning her. He put his arm around her and held onto one breast, pinning her with his leg and burying his face in her hair. He'd staked his claim. She delighted in his protective, dominant stance.

The next morning brought Lady Chantelle Moulton draped on the arm of Lord Peter Gaston, the man who was purported to have written the letter of recommendation for Mrs. Mason.

"I do apologize, Lord Gaston, Lady Moulton, but neither Lord nor Lady Thayer is readily available to receive you. If you will accept their hospitality and wait in the parlor, then I will endeavor to find them," announced the stately Mr. Thorpe. "Shall I send in tea?"

"Yes, that would be excellent. It has been a long, dry morning. I know that they were not expecting us, so we will be happy to await their pleasure."

"Very—"

"I simply need my room, for I am tired and need to freshen up after a short rest. Stephen will not mind that I am here. He never does."

"Excuse me, Lady Moulton, but I wonder if you have not confused Lord Thayer with another. For I have been his butler for as long as he has held his own residence, these last eight years, and I assure you that except for one visit when his lordship was not in residence while still in London, you have never stepped foot in this house. I shall be back presently."

The butler had the two unannounced visitors supplied with a light tea, and he sent several of the staff in search of Lord and Lady Thayer all with the information of the visitors waiting for them in the front parlor. Before too long, both entities arrived, Lord before Lady by mere seconds.

Stephen stopped outside the closed entry and waited for his wife.

"Stephen," Annalise spoke in a stage whisper, "I will not have that woman in my house."

"I agree," he mimicked her whisper, "but if they have traveled all morning, as it appears from my conversation with Thorpe, then they will need to rest and replenish. Besides, I need to speak with Gaston alone. I need to settle upon an understanding with him on the situation, and after which, I will need to have an understanding with Lady Moulton."

"Yes, I would love to come to an agreement with her. Especially about the understanding she appears to have acquired on her own."

"You will do no such thing. You will not cause any trouble and will not even discuss the incident concerning Mrs. Mason or the gossip fiasco here yesterday. You may not even speak of the London visit."

"But—"

"Annalise, I forbid it."

"It isn't at all fair. Then what am I to discuss with that swine?"

"Speak of our guests, our shooting party, the weather, her companion, anything but what you are forbidden to talk about. Do you understand?"

"Yes, I understand. Stephen. Why is it that you always end a sentence in a way that says that I will be punished for violating your edict? If you are dissatisfied the sentence ends with the words, 'do you understand?'"

"So there is no mistake when I redden your backside."

"When?"

"Yes, when. Leesie will be naughty in the near future."

Annalise reached for the handle and Stephen placed his hand over hers and stayed her action as he bent to kiss her warmly. He deepened his voice, "Behave, wife." His wife smiled.

Stephen had been gone for half an hour already, and the conversation surrounding neutral subjects had been exhausted in the front parlor. Annalise was beginning to feel some panic at what the next subjects were going to be when Mrs. Thorpe, bless her heart, knocked and gained entrance bringing with her a replenishment of tea and Lady Charlotte. Annalise smiled her appreciation, moving over for Lottie to sit.

"Lady Raine, how good of you to join us. Are you acquainted with Lady Chantelle Moulton?"

"No, I do not believe I have had the pleasure." Lottie was every inch the Lady at this moment, and Annalise was determined to be that accomplished as well. She still had several more demons to address before peace would reign in her life.

"Well then, Lady Charlotte Raine, may I introduce you to Lady Chantelle Moulton? Lady Moulton, Lady Raine."

"Ah, yes, Lady Moulton, the woman who mistakenly thought she was engaged to your husband, correct?"

Charlotte looked away from Annalise and nodded her head at Lady Moulton, stiffening her posture and tone. "I believe you did mention that unfortunate incident. But it is cleared up now, surely?"

Lady Moulton shifted uncomfortably in her seat. "Yes, that was a miscommunication."

"Yes. I believe that is a dead subject now." Remembering what her husband had admonished her, Annalise tried to steer the subject to other areas.

"Lady Raine, did you go riding this morning?"

"I did, actually. The weather was crisp and perfect for riding. I wish you had attended."

"Yes, well, I had a few things that required my attention. I wanted to ensure our evening entertainment was as planned."

"Well, I shall forgive you, but my companions were quite full of gossip, which took away from my enjoyment."

Lottie turned to Lady Moulton. "Are you acquainted with Lady Jane Whittenbrach?"

"Why yes, how are you acquainted with her?"

"Well, I just became acquainted on this visit. Your friend is here, you know."

Lady Chantelle lost all color in her face and Annalise feared she would faint, but the woman recovered. Lady Charlotte was not put off at all. She continued blithely.

"Yes, do you find her overly chatty about other people's affairs? I mean, she was the soul of indiscretion earlier with Lady Thayer." She turned to Annalise, "Wasn't it something about a Mrs. Mason or some such thing, dear?"

The sound of the clearing of a familiar man's throat interrupted any response from Annalise, and she jumped, and then smiled her relief as she greeted her husband.

"Have you concluded your business, Milord?"

Stephen studied his wife for a few seconds before responding. "Yes, we have completed our business. Lady Charlotte, I believe your husband was inquiring as to your whereabouts. Shall I send word that you are in the front parlor playing a game of cat and mouse?"

"Um, no thank you. I should leave you to it, anyway." She turned to look at Lady Moulton. "Very nice to have made your acquaintance. Perchance we may meet again, dear."

"Ah, yes, possibly." Lady Moulton appeared confused and a little apprehensive.

Lottie leaned into Annalise and said, "Please don't let your husband tell mine I was taunting, for I would dearly like to go riding again tomorrow." She kissed Annalise's cheek and left, darting around Stephen.

"Shall I ring for fresh tea, Lord Thayer, as I take my leave of you?" asked Annalise, anxious to make her own escape.

"No, we have had refreshments in my study. I would like you to stay, my dear."

"Oh, very well," but she moved from the sofa to walk to the window, only to be snagged by the hand and brought to sit beside Stephen on the settee.

There was an uncomfortable silence for what seemed an eternity before Stephen spoke. He wasn't unkind, but it was clear he had something to say of great importance.

"Lady Moulton, some time ago it had come to my attention that you arrived at my home in London unannounced, much like today, stating that you were affianced to me. Is this correct?"

"Yes, but, Stephen, it was but a lark."

"Excuse me, madam, but I do not feel that one previous invitation to a soiree in my home in London, and one dance at the same soiree gives you the familiarity needed to refer to me by my Christian name." Stephen's tone was icy.

Lady Moulton's posture mimicked his tone. "Yes, you are correct."

Lord Peter Gaston entered the fray. "My lady, are you to tell me that you do not even know this man other than to have been introduced during one dance?"

Chantelle did not answer. Stephen continued.

"And am I to understand that you entreated a woman who is already employed as a companion to Lady Whittenbrach's mother to come into my home and try to destroy and discredit my wife?"

Chantelle did reply to that. "All right, since you know, yes, I sent Mrs. Mason to answer your advertisement that Peter so obligingly left on his desk. And the information she was privy to for that week was invaluable."

"I will not speak to the things Mrs. Mason may have said, but I will talk to the several other things. Mrs. Mason came in the late evening and was gone by noon the next morning so any information she may have said she gathered for a week must all be in question as her character certainly is. As for you, I am disgusted at the sight of you. I at first thought you to be a designing piece of baggage after visiting my home and telling my wife you were engaged to me."

"How was I to know she was your wife?"

"How indeed, since your whole story was rubbish. And today, after all the deceitful and dishonest things you have done, you dared to embroil my friends once again, my wife, and my household in your mendacious behaviors. It is untenable. A truly indefensible set of actions.

"I have sent word that you are to be given a room until the morning when you will be escorted from this house and never to return. You are not to leave your room until you leave this house, and if you do, I shall turn you out without regret. You will not say one thing about my wife or my household, or I will make all of these incidents known. I do have the proper connections to ruin you, Lady Moulton. I would recommend you maintain you have never met us."

Annalise, who remained silent throughout the dressing down, jumped when her husband reached for her hand. She realized her hands were cold when his warm one encompassed hers. He must have noticed as well, for he rubbed them tenderly.

"My dear, will you ring for Mrs. Thorpe? I believe she is waiting to take Lady Moulton to her room."

Annalise nodded, for she didn't trust her voice. Happy to move from her seat, she stood to do as Stephen bid, experiencing an intense wave of light-headedness and nausea.

Stephen lept into action and swung her up into his arms, barked to Gaston, "Stay with Lady Moulton until someone comes to get her." Stephen opened the door, yelled for Mrs. Thorpe and shouted at a downstairs maid to get the doctor.

"No, Stephen, I don't need a doctor. I am quite well now. I must have stood too quickly or possibly I need a nap."

"I must have startled you. Yes, possibly a nap is a good idea. For you, it means you are ill."

"Sweetheart," Annalise spoke in low tones, "I am not sick." She leaned close to his ear and whispered, "I am anticipating our first little one."

He stopped dead in the middle of the staircase. "A baby? You are having a baby?" he asked in wonder. "You are having my child. We are starting our nursery. You're sure?"

"Yes, I am absolutely certain and so is Mrs. Thorpe."

"Why didn't you tell me? It was what I have been hoping for."

"You have? I assumed so in London, but you never actually said you were hoping for us to start immediately. I just was certain earlier today, and you have been so busy, I had not found the opportunity until now."

"Well, then you do need a nap, and I need to change our schedule around to accommodate you. Mrs. Thorpe will assist me."

"But not now, dear. We have guests."

"What of it? They will be gone soon."

Annalise knew he was happy, and she snuggled in as he continued up the stairs and into his bedchamber. She would tackle his over exuberance later. For now, she would bask in his love.

Chapter 21

With their guests now gone, the house fell back into their usual routine, to which everyone was thankful. It was several nights later, in the library, that Annalise asked Stephen a question she had been mulling over for a while. Since the fire incident, they spent more time in the library. Annalise knew it was Stephen's way of saying he had not only forgiven her, but that she needed to learn to forgive herself by becoming comfortable in that room. He would help by being in the room with her as often as feasible. She loved this man on deeper levels every day.

"Stephen, Elizabeth has long since given birth, and I can't imagine she hasn't recovered. So why is it that your brother or your parents haven't come to see us again?"

"Ah. I wondered if you were going to ask a question like that at some point. I'm not sure how else to say this, so I'll simply say it. My mother is a snob, and my father does not like to distress her. My brother is out of the country, and Elizabeth cannot reconcile to the fact that a nurse is to relieve her of some of the baby duties, even though it is her second."

"I see. Shall we live the whole of our lives ostracized by them? Are you to be forever separated from your family because of me?"

"It has not a thing to do with you. It has everything to do with my mother's inability to accept my choices. They've spent two years discussing ad nauseam who they felt I should look at and whom I should consider taking to wife. It was amusing until it was no longer entertaining. However, that didn't stop them from continuing their matchmaking. Mother's interference, mostly."

"I don't know how to make this better."

"It is not yours to correct. It is Mother's choices and she will be required to correct them. In fact, the week before I met you, my parents declared my intentions to the world. Every polite and impolite mama and her daughter jockeyed for my attentions. My particular tastes never have, and I imagine, never will be disclosed to my family. Therefore, their offerings laid before me to consider as to acceptability were never going to do. Because of those desires, I required a woman who was not so ingrained in the societal norms that she couldn't enjoy some naughty."

"Like me."

"Yes, and no. I never imagined I could find a treasure like you. I had resigned myself to having to spend years grooming situations around a wife. I was mildly hopeful that she might agree to allow me to coddle her as Leesie does or ravage her as Anna does. The Lady Thayer part being the only understood part of the woman it would not be necessary to train." He leaned down and turned her into his kiss. "You, however, fell into the first two roles without thought. What needed to be trained was some of the Lady Thayer necessities, which are just rules of a presumptuous society created to support their egotistical snobbery. It was the first two parts of the make-up of my wife that would be almost impossible to teach. Those parts required her to feel it deep inside her being."

He drew her closer to him, and he put his chin on the top of her head as he brought her to his chest, arms wrapped tightly around her, almost as though he were protecting her while he rubbed her minimally expanding belly.

"So if you had not impulsively married me, a decision no one would have faulted you for, I wouldn't have created this beautiful life.

In fact, I am sure your peers thought you barmy for considering me as your spouse. That opinion may never change."

"Perhaps, but those who cared might not have liked the person that I chose, no matter who it was. You have to understand I would still have married someone with whom my particular enjoyments were shared. I believe the true point is that it was my choice. I did not harangue James about marrying Elizabeth, although there was some question of her fidelity in their first year of marriage. That was his choice. He chose Elizabeth, and he opted to stay with her. He still chooses her. I don't care because it is their life. Just as ours is private to us. However, I'm not to be afforded the same courtesy, apparently."

His irritation, anger, and hurt clearly evident because he stiffened and loosened his grasp on Annalise, ultimately sitting up and straightening her as well. She watched her husband for a moment and was gratified when he accepted the hand that she offered him and comfort from her bosom.

"It might also be because you are the first son. If it had been James who had married me, the worry wouldn't have been so great." She paused before taking a fortifying breath, blowing it out slowly. "Stephen, are you sorry that you married me?" She almost cried out at the minute hesitation that followed.

"You are everything that I ever wanted in a wife and yet could never find. Oh, I'm sure there were other people out there who would've fit the bill, but none so perfectly as you. I love you."

She heard the sweet words, but she also heard the regret of the circumstances with which they were delivered, and she heard that he avoided the actual question. That question now hung in the air, dark and painful.

They fell silent and soon went up to bed. With nothing more than a few kisses, they took their normal cuddled up position in Stephen's bed and soon she could hear him sleeping. Sleep, however, did not come easily for her. She could not stop worrying about the loss of his family because of his choice to marry her. It was nearly predawn before she finally closed her eyes only to open them again when Stephen awoke, leaving their bed cold and her heart aching.

Today there was significance in him leaving her bed quietly because she mentally added it. He had gone from their bed at this time almost every morning now, confident in the knowledge that he could come back and wake her as he said he loved to do, with his lips. She added extra significance to the fact that they fell asleep last night instead of making love first. She rejected that it was what most couples did. They were not most couples, and it only happened occasionally for them. She ignored that they slept in the same bed all night, which was another area that most did not do. In fact, she did not know of another couple who did, routinely.

Maybe it was time for her to look at returning to London. Even while she thought about it, she knew she couldn't comment on several levels. She loved Stephen and did not doubt he loved her. She didn't know how she would be able to change the lifestyle she had become accustomed to, but she knew that it was possible. Her mother had done it, hadn't she? She wasn't sure she could sacrifice being his wife to give him the freedoms he needed for his family to accept him back. For his mother to draw him back into her good graces.

There was one other thing that she had to think of now that she had confirmed their child. There was now more than a slight increase down near her muff. She had a small, rounded pouch that Stephen kissed and kept his hand on whenever he was able. He was a gentle, loving man no matter the employees and community that relied heavily on the estate of which is was currently co-running with his father and brother.

She would speak to Mrs. Thorpe about timing, but she knew, even as she mourned his loss of family connection, she would need to stay under his protection for their child's sake. She was able to relax, as though knowing she had no choice. Their baby took what would have been a devastating decision away from her. Her relief was profound, and she fell back into a restful sleep.

IT HAD BEEN A MONTH since they had returned from Grimsby. Annalise had been anxious to find a few answers about her parents and the life she was born to. She pulled out the locket and stared at the likeness of her parents. It was hard to tell if they were happy with each other, for the looks were severe. Her mother said they were happy, so Annalise had to believe it to be true. Anna looked up to see her husband enter the bedroom. His face brightened when he spied her in their sitting room. He walked directly to her and placed his hand on her very small belly bump.

"Good Morning, darling. You are sleeping more these days, but I know you are enduring sickness in the morning. Did you have your toast? Are you feeling well today?"

"I understand this is how it is when one is with child. Bigger, slower, more tired, hungrier, and grumpier. And I did not sleep well last night."

He frowned. "I had thought not. I was very tired when I fell into bed. It was late when I finished the paperwork. I apologize that I didn't notice your discomfort. Particularly during the night. Have you eaten today?"

She shook her head. "I haven't yet and your child is complaining."

"Anna, you have to stay on the schedule we have devised. You agreed to do your best."

"And I have, but sometimes life is just off centered. That is it today. I awoke, you were gone, leaving my bed very cold." Her attempt to speak reproachfully was all but ignored.

"I want my wife to sleep in the mornings, but I have responsibilities that cannot wait. Besides, if I am up and working earlier, then I have more time to spend with you."

"I suppose. Ring for my breakfast then, as I no longer am nauseous and find myself starving."

They sat and waited for her food while they cuddled on the cozy lounge sofa and spoke of the trip to Grimsby.

"Are you content with the answers you found about your parents and the items of your history that you now have?"

"Yes, although I would have liked to have the chance to speak to my uncle before he passed. My cousin Robert was more than accommodating. It was nice to reconnect with the places that I was familiar with as a young child. And the paintings are nice to add to the gallery. I do worry about who he is going to sell to. I suppose it won't matter as much, really. I didn't know where the property was until reacquainting with Charlotte."

"Yes, well, I was going to tell you when you gave me my first child, but I can't seem to hold the news."

"I'll remember that if the secret is imperative."

He kissed her hard and grinned. "Minx. The estate is small, and the funds needed to purchase correspond to its size. I had thought to purchase a place in Kent or Cornwall, but this is just as wild and lovely as Cornwall. Because it is changing hands, we will change its name. They have sheep and plenty to keep it productive. I have talked with my partners. We will have one of my smaller ships come in there, creating a small docking port. It will be helpful when I need supplies and the like."

"Stephen, that sounds like a lot of investment."

"Some, but your husband can well afford it, my love. The area will prosper from the added access and since there are more estates near, it will be profitable as well. I have been working on this purchase and arrangements since I heard it was up for sale. Your cousin was more than happy with the outcome. Next week Spritely House will be ours."

"Spritely House? Is that what you named it? How perfectly wonderful." She leaned up to kiss his handsome face. You are perfectly wonderful. I love you so very much. Oh, but how much is it? I mean, should you do that? Won't—"

"You are not to ask a question like that of your husband. You know I would do only what is a good investment, and I have plans for that property. If I can preserve some of your heritage as well, then so be it."

"No questions, my lord."

"I am sorry for your loss of a proper childhood. One you were born to have. I can help with the loss of further birthright this way."

"I'm not sad to have been raised away from there, not now that I know the outcome. You see, if my father had not died, I would have been raised as an elegant lady. Then I would never have met you, and even if I did, I am rather positive that your propensities towards spanking and nurturing so profoundly would have appalled me. I would have been one of those milquetoast women you turned your nose up at."

"I did not turn my nose up at any woman."

"But they didn't fit you as I would not have fit you. So I am happy with the way things have turned out. And glad to know that I am a real lady by birth, even if it doesn't mean too much now, in this present dilemma."

"It means I am grateful for who you are and what joy you have brought into my life. If you were taken from me, I would never survive the loss. It is why I am worried about the birth."

"Do not worry. Mrs. Thorpe says I have 'childbearing hips.' In any other circumstances, I don't think wider hips are an asset, but they are in this case. It means I have plenty of space to accommodate your child."

"Well, if that is the case, I am ecstatic that you are so 'accommodating.' Do you think you could 'accommodate' me now?"

"But my breakfast, milord."

"Just a little taste for me as my breakfast has been worked away," he said as he slipped further down the bed. "Now stay very quiet, my love. We do not want to entertain or scandalize the staff."

His tongue swiped through her slit that was already wet for him. He looked up and smiled at his wife, who had leaned her head back to enjoy his ministrations. He would normally have her watch him give her pleasure but this morning, he needed to be quick about it because her breakfast would come in moments. His staff worked hard to please.

"Mmm, milord," she moaned.

"Quiet, milady, or I will have to punish instead of pleasure."

She grabbed the closest sofa pillow and covered her mouth as her orgasm began to take over. Hard. Fast, satisfying. Stephen wiped his face on his pocket handkerchief.

"Thank you, my love. You are the perfect snack."

The knock on the door was completely ignored by Anna, who still had her head leaned back against the sofa and her eyes closed as she tried to enjoy the last throes of her completion. Stephen was quick to answer the door and take the fully loaded tray.

"Good God man, she won't eat this amount of food."

"Aye, milord, but Mrs. Roundtree felt you might want a bit, for it has been several hours since you've partaken of your own breakfast."

Stephen startled the young footman by laughing heartily. "She is quite right," he said as he sat the laden tray down near his darling. "I will take it from here."

Epilogue

Annalise looked across the large and very crowded ballroom in her home. Stephen had said it would be a crush, and she now knew why. Why anyone would do this purposely, she still had trouble understanding, but Stephen said it was a repayment soirée. It was a thank you for all the invitations they received, regardless of whether they were events they attended or not. They were expected to reciprocate. In truth, Annalise knew it was a party that Stephen wanted to give in response to all of those friends and neighbors who had received them out of hand. Many had accepted their union before his mother, the marchioness, had come around.

Tonight marked the end of her lying-in after the birth of their little boy, Edward Stephen Coton Thayer, two months ago. While Stephen had taken extra measures to make sure that she had waited the full amount of time before reigniting their full relations, she was a woman well cared for and frustration was never endured for long.

Annalise had learned a few things about satisfying her husband as well in the last weeks, and she was as eager as Stephen to end the imposed long wait. She looked at her husband with love and was met with such a look of adoration that it took her breath away. Yes, tonight she was going to play. After the party goers had gone home.

STEPHEN HAD SAID GOODNIGHT to Julian, who now preferred to be called Reese, who in the last months had shown himself to be a good, sturdy boy who enjoyed learning all it meant to be the ward of an earl. His sister still called him Jules when they were alone.

When Annalise had asked if she could try to get the boy, now seven years old, Stephen had been skeptical at first. He wondered what Charles Hayfield would ask for in return. He was surprised that the man had practically handed him over without two words.

Annalise had been just a few months from giving birth, and Stephen was worried that she would overdo things. She hadn't. It was as though she had relaxed and she was even more compliant, in front of the boy, at least. Stephen had learned to use that little fact when necessary. He loved that his Anna needed to show her properly obedient side to the boy because many an argument was circumvented when presented with the boy nearby. It was sneaky, but Stephen bore no guilt over the practice.at

Reese often followed Stephen, doing what he could to emulate him. Stephen knew he was in trouble when Reese entreated him to keep a governess out of the household until he had turned eight. Stephen agreed if Reese learned all he could from the surrounding adults and minded the nanny. Reese had been horrified when he learned there was to be a nanny, but Stephen spoke matter-of-factly when he pointed out the new baby on its way.

"I shall rely on you to teach her how things are done around here so that when your nephew arrives, all will be as it should."

When given that important task, he had taken to the nanny entirely. She allowed his instructions on things and he came to adore her.

When his son was born, Stephen thought he would expire from the joy that his wife and son were healthy. Once the immediate newness had worn off, Stephen had to be content with satisfying his wife in every way she asked so that she would endure the lying-in time that he was determined she would complete.

She had stayed in their chambers and the nursery exclusively for the first month, but the second month found him promising to keep a tally on her disobedience. She simply smiled and handed his son to him as she continued down the stairs into the sitting room, which she had grown exceptionally attached to.

His wonton wife had learned to sate him as well. Something he did not expect from her but was very glad he had not married a debutante or one of the women his mother had chosen for him. Those women, he felt sure, would not allow any position, save the expected way of congress and he and Anna did much more than that. That did not mean that in the last two months he had not been planning and anticipating tonight when she would no longer be his forbidden fruit. He starved for her wet heat around his iron-hard rod.

He marveled at her abilities to still run the household, care for her brother, him, and their infant without losing her cool. Of course, the staff did the majority of the actual work, but she was the commander of the troops, and now he watched her return from nursing their son, weaving herself through the room, looking good enough to ravish.

It was as though she had finally found her place in this world, their world. His mother had been impressed as well, even though she had said nothing. His brother, James, had mentioned to his brother that things might change when their child was born. He had been right. His parents changed their tune about Annalise when their grandson was born, his heir.

Of course, earlier this evening, his mother said, "You aren't safe until you have a spare, dear." He smiled. Before marrying, he hadn't realized that his mother wasn't happy if she wasn't finding something to warn or complain about. So be it so long as she left his Annalise alone to be her happy, exuberant self.

His Lady Thayer did not even blink an eye when she heard her mother-in-law's statement. The minx blithely replied, "You are so right, marchioness. I intend to entice Stephen to lie with me continually until we have several spares. Then we will work on the daughters."

Stephen smiled wickedly. "What an excellent idea, my love. Is it too soon to start tonight?" The marchioness was scandalized and walked off mumbling.

Stephen whispered, "I shall have to punish you for that bit of naughtiness, Anna."

"Oh? Well, I guess you will do what you must, my love," she said as she walked away with a bit more sway than is strictly proper.

He watched as his lovely wife sauntered away to speak with guests, now the consummate hostess. Stephen groaned at the memory of his wanton woman that he would finally have again in a few hours.

He'd asked for her, had paid a bride's price for her, and sometimes just the mention of her name made his cock a bit too responsive at all the wrong moments, but the alternative, he reminded himself, was not worth entertaining.

This woman, his woman, who had conquered his home, his heart and his soul with her child-like innocence, her wanton abandon, and her grace in difficult circumstances, was all he had ever dreamed of and more. This same woman was now the mother of his son. He'd made his choice. She was all he would ever want, ever need.

He would forever be thankful that he had acted impulsively and made the right choice.

"Darling, the guests are gone, and you have fed our son, and he is safe with his nurse."

"Yes, and I believe your wait is over. That is, if you want it to be."

Stephen reached over to help his wife undress from her nightgown and smiled at her eagerness. He was more than ready. It was gratifying to see she was as well. He undressed and placed her gently on the bed, latching onto her milk-enlarged breasts with alacrity.

"I am ready to remind you how much you mean to me," he said as his wife hummed. "You are all I will ever need or want, my Lady Thayer."

"Mmm. I love you, Stephen," she murmured as he switched breasts and her ability to speak was temporarily removed. His desire to speak went the way of her ability, as he loved his wife.

The End

Alyssa Bailey

USA Today and #1 Bestselling Author of Diverse Romance that is realistic and sensual with a touch of suspense. A dyed in the wool Texan living in Alaska for half her life, Alyssa now divides her time between the beauty of Southeast Alaska and the Piney Woods of East Texas. She enjoys taking from her own experiences to create series in fictitious worlds sure to tease the reader's palate and invite them to sink into exciting adventures.

Alyssa enjoys writing consensual power exchanges between intelligent, sassy women who are not afraid to make a stand and loving men confident enough to give his woman space but masterful enough to keep her safe. Whether it is with Cowboys, Military men, Daddies, or Lords, there is *always* a happily ever after.

Visit me online and sign up for my Newsletter:
http://alyssabailey.com
Join my Facebook Group for fun and prizes:
https://www.facebook.com/alyssabailey.romance

Find me on Social Media: https://linktr.ee/alyssabailey

Other Alpha Romance Books by Alyssa Bailey

DARLING DUCHESSES: Regency, Daddy Dom, Spicy
>The Devil Duke's Little Distraction
>The Daring Duke's Little Impulse

LORDS AND LITTLE LADIES-Regency, Benevolent Daddy Dom, Spicy
>Lord Thayer's Choice
>Lord Ashton Decides (Feb 2024)
>The Black Laird Requires (March 2024)
>Lord Kendrick's Obligation (March 2024)

CLEARWATER DADDIES Trilogy -Contemporary, Spicy
>Piper's Plan
>Camille's Second Chance
>Josie's Refuge

LONE WIND SERIES: Contemporary, spicy Native American
>Reclaiming Clover

SAGE COUNTY (Cowboy, Contemporary, Spicy)
>Deep Waters
>Still Waters

GUARDIANS OF REFUGE (Contemporary, Military, Spicy)
SEAL of Refuge
The Strategy of Love
The Tactics of Love
The Mandate of Love

SAFE AND SECURE SERIES: Contemporary, military, suspense, spicy
Saving Sharlee
Saving Jessie
Saving Ivy
Saving Mallory
Saving Callie
Saving Becky
Saving Oakley
Saving Finley
Christmas Boxset
Christmas Wishes and You
The Spirit of Christmas
A Chance of Snow
Anthologies (Heat Varies)
Sweet Town Love
Historical Heroes
Multi-Author Box Sets *(Heat Level Various)*
Love, Christmas 2 Movies You Love
Love, Christmas 2 Recipes
FREE Book Bites 11
Christmas Shorts
Irresistible Heroes
Tempting Protectors
Sexy and Seductive

Sweet and Sassy Summertime Vol. 2
Dear Santa: A Christmas Wish
Sweet and Sassy

Audiobooks
Accepting His Ways
Her Sweet Complication
His Gentle Persuasion
Quinlan's Quest
Lady Caroline's Defiance
Safe and Secure Series

Don't miss out!

Visit the website below and you can sign up to receive emails whenever Alyssa Bailey publishes a new book. There's no charge and no obligation.

https://books2read.com/r/B-A-MXIL-RPLVC

BOOKS 2 READ

Connecting independent readers to independent writers.

Did you love *Lord Thayer's Choice*? Then you should read *The Devil Duke's Distraction* by Alyssa Bailey!

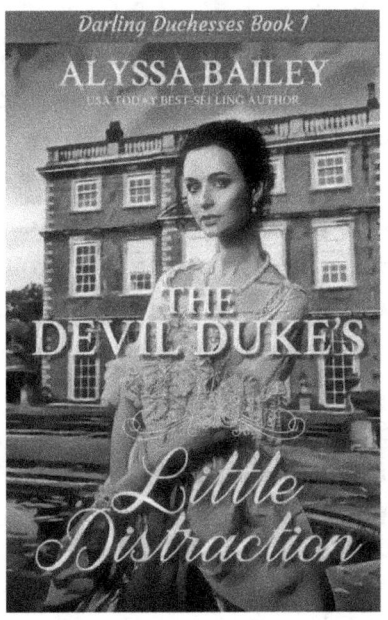

Falling in love was never part of the bargain.

Lady Sofia Cloverfield's family has disintegrated, and she finds herself on the streets to make her own way with only a few guineas and her wits with which to rely on to survive. Sofia uses her common sense and prays she can figure out how to turn her fate around.

Exeter Trenton, the Devil Duke, is wealthy, handsome, and lonely. His position demands he take a wife, but he finds none to his liking. Then, quite by accident, his luck changes when his horses nearly trample a waif he mistakes for a child. He allows her to leave with his chastisement ringing in her ear but not before he finds she is no child.

Once home, Trenton finds he can't get the little minx out of his mind. Telling himself he would be creating a better life for her, he devises a plan to bring her home for a brief distraction.

The Duke initially intends to enjoy her attributes and teach her the thrills of being a woman with an attentive lover. One who engages in incomparable pleasures while remaining diligent in keeping her safe, but plans change, and before he can stop her, his little distraction has gotten under his skin and crawled into his heart.

Now the Devil Duke can never let her go.

Just as Sofia realizes Trenton is more dangerous than she ever suspected, her heart is engaged, and her life is at risk, forcing her to draw on every skill she has learned to save herself from a fate she had barely escaped several times before.

The Duke's goals for Sofia may have changed, but not even the confident, masterful, and influential Duke can see into the future and know that someone else has a different ending planned for his Fia... a very different ending.

Read more at alyssabailey.com.

Also by Alyssa Bailey

Lords and Little Ladies
Lord Thayer's Choice

Watch for more at alyssabailey.com.